"Did you mea

Sean bent to the t[...] only then realizing she'd followed him into the pouring rain when he'd left the car. "Mean what?"

"About this being just the beginning..." Her eyes were huge, her body taut with...nerves?

"I meant it," he said with an ease that no longer startled him. "Now go stay warm in the car."

Instead, she went down on her knees in the dirt beside him, reaching out to stroke away a strand of wet hair from his eyes. "You look very sexy all wet, Sean O'Mara."

"Yeah?"

"Oh, yeah." She bit her full lower lip and Sean promptly dropped the jack.

"If I help with the tire," she whispered in his ear, "we'll get done faster, which would leave us at least a couple of hours' darkness left to do...well, whatever we please."

Sean broke the world record changing the tire, with Carly's soft laughter egging him on.

"My, my," she crooned, handing him the wrench. "A man who can use his tools. I like that."

Dear Reader,

So how many times did you dream of being a princess? Come on, tell me true. I did. Often. Especially when I was little, but mostly that was because I wanted the tiara. As I grew up, the tiara took a back seat to getting Prince Charming. In *A Prince of a Guy*, my heroine, a princess in her own right, wants Prince Charming, too, but she wants him to be a "normal" guy and look at her as if she's a "normal" woman. She gets a whole lot more than that when love enters the fray!

I'm honored to be kicking off RED-HOT ROYALS for Harlequin, and hope you enjoy the entire series, including my 2-in-1 ROYAL DUETS in October!

Happy reading,

Jill Shalvis

P.S. You can write me at www.jillshalvis.com or P.O. Box 3945, Truckee, CA 96160-3945.

Books by Jill Shalvis

A PRINCE OF A GUY
Jill Shalvis

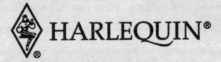

TORONTO • NEW YORK • LONDON
AMSTERDAM • PARIS • SYDNEY • HAMBURG
STOCKHOLM • ATHENS • TOKYO • MILAN • MADRID
PRAGUE • WARSAW • BUDAPEST • AUCKLAND

ISBN 0-373-25961-1

A PRINCE OF A GUY

Copyright © 2002 by Jill Shalvis.

This edition published by arrangement with Harlequin Books S.A.

® and TM are trademarks of the publisher. Trademarks indicated with
® are registered in the United States Patent and Trademark Office, the
Canadian Trade Marks Office and in other countries.

Visit us at www.eHarlequin.com

Printed in U.S.A.

1

IT TOOK Sean O'Mara a full five minutes to realize he was being taken advantage of, maybe six. His only defense was that he'd worked until past midnight and it was barely five in the morning, leaving him bleary-eyed and bewildered.

"You're...what?" he asked again slowly, trying to make sense of the whirlwind that had barged into his house.

"I'm going to England for two weeks." His sister deposited her four-year-old daughter, Melissa, on the floor of the foyer where Sean stood. The little girl immediately vanished into his kitchen. His sister vanished, too, only to return twice, each time with a huge load from her car.

Not a good sign. "England?" he asked, getting less groggy by the passing minute.

"Yep." She said this as if it was only across the street from his Santa Barbara, California home, instead of across the globe.

"I can't tell you how much your help

means to me, Sean." She staggered beneath an armful. "Melissa'll be no trouble, I promise, and I'll finish the design job ASAP."

Melissa, no trouble? *Ha!* That had to be some sort of oxymoron. Exhaustion was quickly replaced by a gnawing sense of urgency to talk his sister out of this. He couldn't be responsible for a child for two long weeks, he just couldn't. He had work, he had a life...okay, maybe not a life outside of work, but he did have work, plenty of it.

Besides, and most importantly here, he had no idea how to care for a kid.

"Oh, and don't forget," Stacy warned. "She still needs a little help in the bathroom with the, um, paperwork."

"What? Wait a sec." He rubbed his temples. He yawned. He stretched, but he didn't wake up in his own bed, which meant he wasn't dreaming. "You can't just leave her here."

"Why not? You're responsible. You know how to cook. You're kind. Well, mostly. What could go wrong?"

"Anything! Everything!" He struggled for proof and hit the jackpot right in front of him. "I can't even keep goldfish," he said earnestly. "They die. Look." He pointed to the ten-gallon glass aquarium sitting on a table in the entranceway. Empty. "I forget to feed them. So really, that knocks out both the responsible and the kind thing all in one shot."

Stacy's smile was indulgent. "You're going to be fine. Oh, and don't forget to put the toilet seat down or she'll…go fishing."

"But…" Sean craned his neck to peek into his kitchen. On the floor sat a sweet-looking, innocent-seeming child of four years.

He knew better.

Melissa, no matter how golden-curled, was no innocent. She could create a mess faster than he could blink. In her short lifetime, she'd bitten him three times, cut his hair twice—without permission—and peed on his bed only fifteen minutes before a hot date.

The little monster in question, the one who would be no trouble, looked right at him and smiled guilelessly…as she tipped her sipper cup upside down, shaking grape juice all over both her and the clean floor.

The ensuing purple sticky splatters caused her to giggle uproariously.

Fear curled in Sean's belly. "I've got work," he said to Stacy, sounding desperate even to his own ears. But children weren't his thing. He was an architect. He ran his own business, which meant on a good day he put in fourteen hours minimum.

Not surprisingly, he came from a long line of workaholics. Both his grandfather and father had been attorneys, great ones, but they'd never spent any time with their children, which was one of the reasons Sean didn't have any.

He had no intention of neglecting *his* children—if he ever had any. Work was everything to him, and so was being the best at what he did.

He could hardly be the best child minder when he had no experience.

"News flash," Stacy said. "You work too darn hard."

"I like my work."

"Uh-huh. And we all know it." Her eyes softened with affection. "When was the last time you had a day off?"

"Well..." He couldn't remember exactly, but thought it had probably been about two years ago when his ex-fiancée had nearly destroyed him.

"I'm doing you a favor, Seany, you'll see. Melissa will show you how wonderful life is, or how it could be if you'd only slow down for a moment and take a deep breath.

As it is now, you wouldn't know how to enjoy life if it bit you on the tush."

It didn't take a rocket scientist to know he was losing this battle. "But—"

"Just try it, Sean. Do a puzzle. Color in a coloring book. It's a terrific stress reliever."

Color in a coloring book? Sean shuddered at the thought, but there was something to his sister's voice beyond the coaxing. Something...desperate? "Stace? What's really the matter here?"

She ignored the question, put her hands on her hips, blew a tuft of hair from her eyes and surveyed the mountain of gear she'd deposited. "Portable bed. Sipper cups. Clothes for an assortment of weather and activities. Car seat. Booster chair. Life vest for the beach. Humidifier, just in case."

In case of what? "Stacy—"

"Yep, I think that's everything. Oh, and here's a list of numbers you might need." She handed him a stack of business cards. "Doctor, hospital, dentist, insurance company, insurance agent—"

Good God. But beyond his panic, hers had taken root, and it stopped him cold. "Hey." He took her shoulders and forced her to look at him. "What's going on?"

She tried to smile. "I've already told you."

"Just work?"

"Really." Lifting two fingers, she smiled. "Scout's honor."

"Then there's got to be someone else Melissa could stay with, a friend maybe, or—" Even as his words trailed off, he knew the truth. It was all over his sister's face.

She had no one else to ask, no one else to go to.

Their parents had been gone for three years now. His dad of a heart attack, probably from a combination of working eighteen-hour shifts, smoking two packs a day and eating fast food at every turn. His mother had died the same year from pneumonia.

As for friends, Stacy had plenty, just not the responsible kind, as Sean knew all too well, since he'd spent the past few years getting her on the straight and narrow path again.

Dammit, he *knew* she had no one else. Her old friends couldn't be trusted, her new friends were too new. Melissa's father was long gone.

She had no one but him.

Stacy's eyes were solemn, her smile gone.

She was trying so hard to be brave, to get past her tromped on, damaged heart and make it on her own without too much help from her big brother, and what was he doing?

Trying to turn her away.

He couldn't, not after all she'd been through. And since he loved her with all his own damaged heart, he sighed. "It's okay." He managed a smile. "I'll do it."

"Really?" Her entire face beamed with happiness and a good amount of relief as she flung herself into his arms. "I owe you," she whispered, then blew a kiss to her daughter as she took off toward the door. "Love you, Melissa! Love you, too, Sean!"

And just like that, he was on his own.

He watched her drive off, listening to Melissa's gales of giggles as she did God-only-knew-what to his kitchen. "Love you, too," he said to the quickly disappearing car.

Slowly, dreadfully, he headed into his kitchen.

Melissa smiled and held up her empty juice cup. "More."

Sean rubbed his eyes, then got a sponge and his first life lesson for the day—grape juice stains. Everything. Permanently.

TWO DAYS LATER, Sean's eyes were gritty from lack of sleep. He hadn't touched a razor or done laundry, and his house looked like a cyclone had hit it. Unable to go into his downtown office and baby-sit at the same time, he'd had another phone line installed and was doing what he could from home.

Which amounted to nothing other than chasing a certain four-year-old nightmare.

At the moment, his fax line was ringing, as well as both the regular phones, along with his head. Melissa had insisted on crawling into his bed every hour or so. All night long. Every night.

He suddenly realized that, in sharp contrast to the ringing, the kid was far too quiet.

"Melissa?" he called as he headed toward the phone.

Silence.

The last time she'd been this quiet, she'd been busy pouring liquid bubbles on his hardwood hallway floors, because it made them pretty. He'd hit the hall at a run and went skating on his butt, which had put Melissa into hysterics.

He hoped against hope that his ad in the paper—*desperately seeking two-week nanny*—worked. He hoped today's nanny interviewee showed. He doubted it.

No one else had.

"Melissa" he called again, grabbing the first phone line. It was his harassed secretary, Nikki.

"Well, look at that. He lives," she said into his ear. "Look, I have three contracts for you to go over, five new sets of plans to review and—"

"Hold on." Ignoring her exasperated sigh, he clicked to the second ringing line, which was his latest client, Sam Snider.

As he did this, the fax came alive. Nikki, ever so creative, was faxing the first page of one of the contracts that needed his attention. Sean greeted Sam, skimmed the contract and cocked his free ear for any sign of Melissa, of which there was none.

He'd become the master of multitasking.

"Your design?" he said to Sam. "I should have it ready by—"

"Uncle Sean!" This from the bathroom. Melissa had surfaced.

Hastily covering the phone with his palm, he called, "I'll be right there!"

"Come now, Uncle Sean!"

"I'll be right there," he repeated and uncovered the receiver to continue talking to his client. "As I was saying—"

"But Uncle Sean! I'm done!"

Great. She was done. He tried to put Sam on hold, but the man was long-winded, so he ended up with the man talking in one year and Melissa shouting in the other.

The fax machine continued to spout his contract.

"Uncle Sean!"

Because apparently he wasn't overwhelmed enough, the doorbell rang.

He needed a clone.

Or a wife.

Just two years ago, he'd come close to that with Tina. He'd never regretted not walking down the aisle, not once.

Until now.

Sam kept talking.

"Wipe me!" yelled Melissa, loud enough for the entire county to hear.

"I'll wipe you in a sec!"

Sam sputtered, then said, "Excuse me?"

Sean dropped his head and thunked it on the counter, but even a near concussion didn't change facts. He was failing, pathetically. And failing was the one thing he couldn't handle. Slowly, he counted to ten, but yep, his life was still in the throes of hell.

He politely hung up on his very wealthy client. Then, mourning the loss of that income, he headed into the bathroom and handled Melissa's paperwork.

Together they headed toward the front door. "I hope it's my mommy," Melissa said, bounding in front of him like an eager puppy, her blond curls wild and neglected. She hadn't let Sean near her with a brush since she'd arrived.

He had, however, made her brush her teeth. That must count for something.

"I really want my mommy."

"I know." Sean missed her mommy too. Big time. "But she's not coming home for two weeks. The person at the door wants to be your nanny during the day." *Please, God.*

Melissa stopped short. "How long is two weeks?"

"Fourteen days."

She tilted her head at him, piercing him with huge, baleful eyes. "That's too long."

No kidding. "It'll be over before you know it, kiddo. Do you want to open the door?"

She brightened at that. "I hope it's Mary Poppins. She sings pretty."

Sean didn't care about singing, pretty or otherwise. He needed help on this daddy gig, and he needed it now.

He hoped for an older nanny, a grand-motherly type who had lots of hugs and kisses and stories, all the stuff he didn't have time for. Then he could get back to work without guilt.

Together they opened the door.

"Hello," said the woman who stood there, who was neither old nor Mary Poppins-like.

Sean's first thought was she had the most unusually bright blue eyes he'd ever seen, magnified as they were behind glasses as thick as the bottom of a soda bottle. They sparkled when she smiled, which she was doing right now. And it wasn't a forced, I-need-a-job smile, either, it was the sweetest, most open smile he'd ever seen. Helplessly, he responded to it with one of his own, though his was definitely more from profound relief than anything else.

"I'm Carly Fortune, prospective nanny," she said, tossing her long dark hair over her shoulder as she held out her hand.

"I'm Sean O'Mara, nanny seeker." She wasn't what he'd imagined, not at all, he thought, shaking her warm, soft hand. For one thing, she was young. Her dark hair had fallen in her face again, but mid-twenties was his guess. She wore a long sweater over a wide skirt that fell to her ankles, exposing a pair of chunky boots.

Not an inch of her below her neck showed, so he couldn't tell if she was small, large or somewhere in between. And because he was a man, and mostly a very weak man, at that, he usually noticed a woman for her appearance. Not that he felt particularly proud of that fact, but it was the truth. A beautiful woman turned his head.

Not that this woman wasn't beautiful. More like Sandra Bullock in *Miss Congeniality* before the makeover.

But compassion and joy shimmered from her every pore, and he figured both those personality traits were important when it came to taking care of a child, which was the point to her standing there smiling at him.

And yet the feeling that she was hiding behind her slightly oversize clothing made him uncomfortable. *Tina,* he thought with a flash of bitterness. Two years since the woman who couldn't tell the truth to save her life, and he was *still* second-guessing every woman he came into contact with.

Even so, when she continued to look at him, smiling that infectious, open smile, something very odd happened. From the region of his deadened heart came a pitter-patter, one he nearly failed to recognize.

Then she bent for a large canvas bag at her

side, pushing at her glasses when they nearly slipped off her nose, and through the slit in her too full skirt he saw a flash of long, toned, smooth pale thigh.

Beneath that awful bulk of clothing, one would expect to find more clothing, not...bare lovely skin.

And without warning, the pitter-patter in his heart moved southward.

"But...you're not Mary Poppins." Melissa's lower lip came out, trembled. Her eyes filled, and she ducked behind Sean, clutching the backs of his legs. "I really wanted Mary Poppins." Her voice was muffled as she pressed her face against him, her fingers biting into his skin.

Sean reached back and tried to pry her off, but her fingers only dug in deeper. He wrapped an arm around her small shoulders, thinking that for such a tyrant, she seemed so tiny, so defenseless. No matter. This had to be done. He needed help.

He needed escape.

"Oh, sweetie." Carly glanced at Sean, then kneeled to Melissa's level. "I'm so sorry. You're right, I'm not Mary Poppins. But I do have a really cool carryall like she did, with fun stuff in it, see?" She lifted the canvas bag and shook it enticingly. Something tinkled, something rattled.

Melissa sniffed, then peered around Sean's legs. "Is my mommy in there?"

"Well...no." Her voice was low and husky. Another contradiction. A voice dripping with sensuality in a body dressed for nunhood. "But I've got some dress-up clothes. What do you think?"

Melissa blinked slowly, then nodded. "Okay."

Okay. She'd said okay. Sean found himself grinning stupidly at the woman who was going to save his life.

Or at least the next two weeks of it.

2

FOR THE FIRST TIME in her twenty-six years, she hesitated. But this had been what she wanted, a break from her crazy, whirlwind life. A chance to see how the other half lived.

An opportunity to go slumming.

So Princess Carlyne Fortier stepped into Sean O'Mara's house. Only she didn't do it as an elegant, sophisticated, classy princess. No, she entered as…Carly Fortune.

Her own doing. She regularly scanned newspapers from the United States. It was a habit, much like the way she secretly hoarded and watched old American television shows. Long unsatisfied with her life, she'd been reading the want ads, fantasizing about settling down in relative obscurity, about finding Mr. Right.

It couldn't happen in her world. There were no Mr. Rights in her world, at least none in her immediate future. But she wondered…how was she ever going to get the chance to see if she'd make a good mother?

In light of that, holding a small paper from Santa Barbara, California, an ad had leaped out at her. *Dared* her. Sean O'Mara's nanny ad.

"Do you know how to make play dough?" Melissa asked her.

Oh, boy. Not only was she currently dressed far worse than any example from the don't do this list, she was impersonating an American, an everyday American nanny of a four-year-old girl!

A four-year-old girl who was blinking at her very solemnly.

Carlyne knew nothing about children and even less about making play dough, but that was going to change. "I'm afraid not, but I know where to buy it." And only because she'd happened to see it at K mart while choosing her new unflashy, unsophisticated, un-princess-like attire. She'd fallen in love with the store, where one could buy panty hose and patio furniture from the same place. "It comes in all sorts of colors," she said, proud to be in the know. "And I bet it's better than the homemade stuff, anyway."

"But my mommy makes it," Melissa said, her lower lip sticking out a mile.

No problem. Carlyne would just call

Francesca, her assistant, and have her hunt up a recipe ASAP. She could do this!

"Melissa, play dough isn't required," Sean told her, bending his tall form down to her eye level.

"I want play dough!"

"We've discussed this, remember?" Sean asked. "Yelling at me is not acceptable."

"What's sepable?"

Sean closed his eyes and plowed his fingers through his dark hair. "This is our nanny needer, Melissa," he said to Carlyne, reminding her that this was a job interview.

Not that she needed the money or a place to stay. She had homes in St. Petersburg, Paris and on the coast of Spain. No, what she needed was a chance to live without the silver spoon in her mouth. No doubt, this job would thrust her right into what she imagined normal, middle-American women did every day, and that was what she wanted more than anything. A chance to go to the grocery store, to run her own errands. A chance to go somewhere, anywhere, without light bulbs going off in her face. A chance to see if motherhood agreed with her. She figured America was her best shot, since it was a place known for independence and freedom, two things she wanted with all her heart.

Sean was looking at her with eyes the color of a clear mountain sky, eyes that seemed to see right through her disguise, though she knew that was impossible.

She was no less than the granddaughter, daughter, sister and niece of one of the few royal families left in existence, from a long line of first Russian then French aristocrats. Not many could imagine a more fairytale-like beginning, her family being Russian royalty, then fleeing their country when the empire collapsed. They escaped with their wealth and titles intact and had lived in prosperity in France ever since. She was a princess without a kingdom, a citizen of the world, but because of the fame, never a normal one. People were fascinated by her and her family, and yet not a soul had recognized her on the trek over here. Thanks to her impeccable education and late-night television habit, she spoke flawless English.

She'd donned a long dark wig and had used a heavy hand applying makeup, all to hide her perfect blond bob and flawless, porcelain skin. The sky-blue contacts helped, too, as her mossy-green eyes were distinctive, recognizable. Adding the thick-rimmed glasses had been pure inspiration on her part, except they kept slipping off her nose, which was annoying.

The blue-light-specials outfit had completed the disguise, since Carlyne had never been caught in public in anything less than designer duds.

Well, she was in the public eye now, wasn't she? And on her own without the bodyguards, the buzz of the paparazzi. Grinning with the freedom of it all, she stepped into Sean's mirrored foyer and...stopped short. The sight of her reflection beaming from the wood-framed mirrors left her frozen in shock.

It was one thing to carefully, secretly plan the badly needed "get away to prove herself" escapade.

It was another entirely to look it in the face.

But for too long she'd been feeling disturbingly disconnected. Lonely. Not that anyone in their right mind would feel sorry for her. After all, Princess Carlyne Fortier had everything. Decent looks. A good brain. Wealth. But her looks and wealth were inherited, and come to think of it, so were all her friends—as they were *family* friends. Her brain was courtesy of the best education money could buy. Every single waking moment, she was surrounded by people who needed one thing or another from her, yet no one in her family took her seriously enough to let her do so much as have her own job. She was a lovely ornament. No more, no less.

If things had been different, she wondered, if she'd been born poor or merely an average citizen, who would she be? A regular woman with a regular family—a child?

So was it any wonder she'd packed a bag, dumped all her credit cards—okay, all but one—given herself a hideous makeover and had answered Sean O'Mara's ad?

But Lord, she really had done it...she looked *very* normal.

"Is everything okay?" Sean O'Mara asked her.

His reflection appeared at her side. His nearly black hair fell to his collar and looked as if maybe he'd forgotten to brush it that morning. His polo shirt was untucked, and he had what looked like a fresh stain across his chest. A chest that was very well defined and broad, she couldn't help but notice. His khaki pants were clean, but wrinkled where the wide-eyed little Melissa gripped his long, long legs for all she was worth. His feet were bare, which would normally be a huge turn-off for her, because Carlyne liked and appreciated men who were well dressed from head to toe.

But Sean's feet were tanned and...some-how...sexy.

So were his deep blue eyes, which were fixed on her. He looked curious, probably wondering why she'd been staring in the mirror for the past five minutes.

"Uncle Sean!"

But Uncle Sean was still looking at Carlyne. "I have to be honest," he said quietly. "I'm not sure how to conduct this inter-view."

"That makes two of us." She didn't know how to get a job. She'd never had to prove herself before.

A day for firsts, she decided.

"Uncle Sean!"

"We could start by sitting down." He awkwardly patted the little girl on her back in a way that conveyed his bafflement. Ob-viously, he was not a natural with children. "Did you bring a résumé or references?"

Thank God for her assistant's special tal-ents. Francesca had not only gotten her a used clunker of a car to drive while here, she'd manufactured Carly a résumé and references that would hold up against the tightest scrutiny. "I did," she said with a smile meant to charm and disarm. "But you should know, I've never been a live-in nanny before." She'd never been a live-in *anything* before. Not because she was only twenty-six, but because no man had ever been able to stir her heart enough to encourage her to try.

She'd found it impossible to find a date, much less her soul mate, while constantly surrounded by people, all of whom wanted to be with her simply because of who she was.

"This must be a live-in position," Sean told her. "Melissa belongs to my sister, who's out of town for now. And—" He lowered his voice, and she found the growl that came out very sexy. "I'm really losing it here. I haven't a clue what I'm doing. I need help, fast."

"You're not married?" she asked without thinking, then wondered what he would make of that question.

She didn't know what to make of that question.

"No," he said very firmly, as if the thought were abhorrent. "Not married. Which is why I might need help at night if I have a meeting." He glanced at Melissa as if she were a puzzle missing some pieces.

Carlyne knew the song and dance. She remembered her own nanny well. And the cook. And the maid. During her childhood she'd seen only servants, rarely her own parents, and certainly not during the evening hours when they'd been busy with one social function or another.

She didn't know anything else, but couldn't contain her strange sense of disappointment that this man seemed to be no different.

"You have plenty of experience," Sean said, skimming the list of her supposed previous jobs. "And you have a teaching credential, too."

She had quite a few credentials, and no less than three accredited degrees. She collected them like others collected shoes, mostly because she had yet to figure out what she wanted to do with her life.

"Impressive references," he murmured, and Carlyne sent a silent message of thanks to her assistant for providing the names. "Can you tell me about yourself?" He lifted his head, piercing her with those mesmerizing eyes.

There was a lock of hair over his forehead.

He had a five o'clock shadow. By looks, he could have been a rebel, but the careful way he was reading her résumé seemed at odds with that. "What would you like to know?"

"Well…" He looked confused, as if he wasn't sure exactly. "How about your family? Or how you grew up?"

"Oh, same old thing," she said lightly. Poor little princess. Absent parents. No siblings. No close friends. Nothing she could tell him, of course.

"Really?" Lord, his eyes were deep. "What's the same old thing?"

Since she couldn't explain, she reverted to her lifelong fantasy. "A house with a white picket fence, two parents, various kids and a dog."

"That sounds nice." She could tell he really meant it. "So what makes you want to do this?" He was still looking at her, full of genuine interest and curiosity, as if he really cared.

Carlyne had to swallow hard because a wave of guilt nearly drowned her. She'd been describing her imagined ideals, but that didn't make her lies right.

Another first, for Carlyne never felt guilty about anything.

"Uncle Sean!" The impatient little girl

tugged hard on Sean's shirt, letting it go so that it bounced up, exposing a good portion of lean, flat, tanned belly.

And just like that, Carlyne forgot what she'd been about to say.

"Just a minute, Mel," Sean said distractedly, pushing down his shirt and waiting for Carlyne—Carly—to answer.

But she couldn't, because she just realized what she was doing. She wanted a job working for this man, this gorgeous man, whom she would have to live with for the next two weeks.

Live with, as in play house.

"Carly?"

It took her another minute to remember he was talking to her, because never in her life had she allowed her name to be shortened. She'd never had a nickname. "I want to do this because…" She looked him in the eyes and gave up pretense, telling him the complete, utter truth. "Because I really need to."

"You need to," he repeated.

His gaze filled with compassion, and she winced inwardly, knowing he pictured her destitute and homeless or something equally horrible, which couldn't be further from the truth. "I want this job with all my heart and soul," she said, hoping her earnestness would be enough, that someday if he learned the truth, he'd forgive her. "I'll take good care of Melissa and see that she gets everything she needs."

"You might want to think about this," he said. "Because believe me..." He pulled his stained shirt away from his chest. The material stuck to his skin until the last possible second, letting go with a suctioning sound that for some reason tugged at a place low in Carlyne's belly.

"Grape juice," he muttered. "It's not an easy thing, caring for a four-year-old, so please, be sure. I need total concentration for my work, and she's—" A little guiltily, he looked into Melissa's eyes.

"A nightmare," Melissa said proudly, nodding. "That's what my mommy says."

Sean laughed, the sound rich and genuine, and again, something pulled within Carlyne.

What was the matter with her? She'd heard a man laugh before, for crying out loud. Men far more sophisticated than Sean O'Mara. Smoother, richer, even more good-looking.

But there was something about this man who was obviously unconcerned about opening the door with bare feet and disheveled hair. Something unpolished and edgy. He didn't care what others thought.

Another first for her. All the men in her life cared a great deal for what others thought.

"I'm not sure that's something to be proud of, you know," Sean told Melissa. "Being a nightmare."

"Yes, but Uncle Sean—"

"Hold on, I'm still talking to Carly." He looked at her. "Do you really want the job?"

For some reason, one Carly didn't want to examine too closely, she wanted to stay more than ever. "Yes."

Sean let out a ragged, relieved breath. The weight of the world seemed to lift off his shoulders. "Good."

Awkwardly, they stared at each other.

"Uncle Sean!" Melissa tugged at him again. "I really have to go potty!"

"Again?" Sean turned that steady, heart-skipping gaze on his little niece, who'd let go of his legs to do what was apparently the got-to-go dance, which consisted of holding herself between the legs and skipping around in a little circle.

"Quick!" she demanded.

"You know how to do it."

Still gripping herself, she shifted from foot to foot. "I want you to come with me."

"Melissa—"

"I'm going to have an accident!" she cried, bouncing. "You'd better hurry!"

Groaning, Sean scooped her up. "Be right back," he said to Carlyne, striding away. "Make yourself comfortable."

They headed down the hall, Melissa in her uncle's arms, her beaming face close to his. "I drank too much juice," she confided.

"How could that be? I'm wearing more than half of it."

"I didn't mean to spill."

"Yes, you did." Their voices faded. "You were mad because I wouldn't give you salami for breakfast, remember?"

Carlyne couldn't help herself, she laughed, which was odd as she wasn't one for spontaneous laughter.

Sean stopped, turning to look at her.

He had the longest eyelashes. That was her inane thought. Long and thick and black. Totally wasted on a man. Except that they emphasized the leanness of his cheekbones, the straight line of his nose, his generous mouth, and when he smiled, when those eyes of his closed slightly, his long lashes gave him a sleepy and undeniably sexy look.

She wondered if women fell all over themselves when he smiled like that. If he even knew it.

Of course he knew it. In her experience, men were very aware of themselves. Too aware.

Carlyne didn't plan on falling at his feet, no matter how her heart fluttered. She wasn't here to make friends—or lovers for that matter. She was here to prove something to herself.

But Sean wasn't what she planned on, and he sure wasn't going to be easy to ignore. Unaccustomed nerves leaped at her. "Is the job really mine?"

Melissa bounced in Sean's arms, and with an ease that assured her of his strength, he shifted her to his other side so he could look directly into Carlyne's eyes. "It's yours," he said. "For better or worse."

"Hurry, Uncle Sean, hurry!"

Carlyne had to smile at the pure terror that crossed Sean's face—her father had never, ever given a thought to helping his children in the bathroom—before Sean whirled and rushed down the hall.

No, Sean may not like this responsibility

he'd taken on, but he appeared to be a man who wouldn't shirk his duties. Carlyne watched him with new eyes and an awareness she hadn't expected to feel.

When they were out of sight, her bemused smile slowly faded. She blinked at her reflection, wondering about what she'd done.

Urgent potty calls?

Salami for breakfast?

She shivered at the thought, but then she pictured Sean, all that disturbing dark sensuality, his intensity, and shivered all over again.

AT HIS FIRST opportunity to work without the interruption of a high-strung four-year-old, Sean sat at his desk. He meant to dig in but found himself staring out the window instead.

Melissa was running as fast as her short, chunky legs would take her. Hair flying out behind her, wide, mischievous grin on her face.

Sean rose, swearing, thinking she was on the run from whatever terrible thing she'd done to the new nanny, when said new nanny appeared in the window, as well.

Hair flying behind her, running, and

though he doubted her legs were short and chunky like Melissa's, he couldn't say for certain as they were hidden beneath her skirt. Just like his niece, she wore a wide and mischievous grin, and there was something in her infectious laughter that made him smile, too. She wasn't beautiful, but she was incredibly…real. He liked real.

He liked her.

"Can't catch me, can't catch me," squealed Melissa, slowing with a hopeful, expectant glance over her shoulder.

She wanted to be chased.

She wanted to be caught.

And Sean stood there with a sudden pit in his stomach, because he couldn't remember a single time over the past days that he'd spared the time to play with the little girl like that. Couldn't remember not being annoyed or tired or frustrated.

Couldn't remember laughing, or just… being.

"Can't catch me," Melissa sang.

Catch her, Sean willed Carly, leaning close as if he could do it from the other side of the glass. *Do for her what I never did.*

At the same moment he wished it, Carly surged forward and scooped the little girl up in her arms, swinging her around and around, looking young and happy and free.

Their joined laughter rang out, and finally, they both collapsed in a fit of giggles to the grass. Melissa crawled into Carly's lap.

Carly's arms lifted, and for a second hovered in the air as if she wasn't used to such easy affection, but then she wrapped them around the child, her face filled with such contentment it almost hurt to look at her.

Sean sat down, still watching. Still... yearning?

No, that made no sense. No sense whatsoever.

"SO WHO'S IN CHARGE of dinner?"

Sean lifted his gaze off the plans he'd been studying, the plans he'd been trying to finish since Melissa had stepped into his life, turning it upside down. Slowly he blinked Carly into focus.

She was standing in the doorway of his office, looking quite a bit more rumpled then when she'd arrived for her interview that morning. He knew without asking that the dirty smudges on her wide skirt were from grubby four-year-old hands, that the wrinkles in her shirt came from lifting that same four-year-old, and likely her hair was rioting around her face because of something Melissa had done.

But somehow, she looked...cute. He knew from having a sister, and also a fair amount of relationships, that the word *cute* wasn't exactly considered flattering, but he thought it should be.

What made her so attractive that he couldn't tear his eyes off her? He hadn't a clue.

"Dinner?" she repeated, pushing those huge glasses closer to her eyes. "Melissa's hungry."

"Sure. What are you making?"

She gave him a long, baleful look. "I wasn't offering to make it."

"Oh." The radio at his elbow switched from good old-fashioned rock music to the news.

"And on the celebrity front," the announcer said. "It's rumored that Princess Carlyne Fortier has gone AWOL. Her grandfather denies this, claiming his granddaughter has merely left for a private vacation, but for the first time in ten years the princess didn't attend the International Muscular Dystrophy fund-raiser, held last night in D.C."

Carlyne let out a sound of annoyance, so Sean turned the volume down. "Is it dinnertime already?" he asked.

"Yes." She glared at the radio, which continued to spit out the top-breaking story, very softly now.

"Rumor has it she is close to a nervous breakdown from her heavy social schedule," claimed the announcer, sarcasm in his voice. "Must be a tough life, folks, huh?"

"He hasn't a clue," Carly muttered.

Because she was obviously agitated, Sean flicked the radio off. "Uh, where were we?"

She sighed. "Dinner."

"Yeah. To tell you the truth, I was kinda hoping you could cook." Sean tried his most charming smile.

She merely arched an eyebrow, looking suddenly very aristocratic. "Was cooking in my job description?"

"Well, no." His charming smile was clearly rusty—he hadn't tried to charm a woman in a good long while. He was about to give wheedling a shot when the doorbell rang.

His new nanny sent him a smile every bit as charming as his own—and just as manipulative. "I'll make you a deal," she said, already backing away. "I'll get the door, *you* get dinner going."

"Not a fair trade," he called, rising from his chair, listening as her laughter floated toward him.

"First one to the door," she called tauntingly.

A challenge. He loved challenges. He raced down the hallway after her, enjoying the way her far-too-big skirt flew up, flashing him his second view of her legs. Why she wanted to hide them was a complete mystery.

But then again, most *women* were mysteries.

With his long strides, he could have easily overtaken her, but he got distracted by those legs, so she hit the front door a fraction of a second before he did. Whirling, she pressed her back to the wood, twisting to laugh at him.

To stop his motion, his arms came out automatically, his hands landing on either side of her head to avoid crushing her against the wood.

Both of them were laughing like little kids.

Until his body brushed hers. Time stopped as he stared wide-eyed at her, stricken by the strange electrical current that ran through them.

She seemed similarly conflicted.

Being pressed against a woman wasn't a new experience. Yes, it had been awhile, but not *that* long. Not long enough for him to be holding himself utterly still in order to get a better feel of all those warm curves he could feel beneath her clothes. And not just warm curves, but really great warm curves.

Breasts smashed into his chest. Soft feminine hips pressed to his own. Not an inch of space between them. That combined with the real fact of already being attracted to her as a person caused a very base reaction, and she couldn't have missed it.

Her eyes went wide.

Nope, she didn't miss it. No more than he missed the way her nipples hardened to two tight tips, drilling through all her layers into his shirt.

She felt amazing. Her mouth opened, but the only sound to escape was a little sigh he would have sworn was the sound of helpless awareness. Arousal.

And he couldn't help it. He lowered his head just a fraction, so his mouth nearly touched hers. She was a near stranger, but he needed to kiss her more than he needed his next breath. Given the way she angled her head and parted her lips, she felt the same way.

The doorbell rang again.

Slowly Sean pulled back, his chest, his belly, his thighs leaving hers reluctantly.

She made that little sound again, the one that tugged at him so primally. Hardly able to think, he pulled open the door.

Mrs. Trykowski, Slovak immigrant, next-door neighbor and local pest, brushed past him and marched right on in without being asked.

The eighty-something woman was barely five feet tall, walked with a little skip in her step and had a voice like a truck driver's. "Brought you some fruitcake," she barked in the gravelly, heavily accented voice that assured everyone she'd been smoking like a fiend for over half a century.

She brought Sean fruitcake on a regular basis. Not because he couldn't feed himself, but because the woman had a curiosity streak a mile long.

True to form, she craned her neck down the hallway, looking for new and exciting clues to his life.

Then she spotted Carly.

"Ah," she said, a secret smile on her lips. She winked at Sean.

"Stop it," he said. "Stop it right now."

"I do not know what you are talking about," she said innocently, her narrow, sharp gaze on Carly.

Sean groaned, knowing what was coming—

"Ten," she said triumphantly.

She had a terrible habit of rating his dates. "Mrs. Trykowski, Carly isn't—"

"What does she mean, ten?" Carly asked him.

"Nothing," he assured her, giving his nosy, bossy neighbor the evil eye. "Carly Fortune is Melissa's new nanny for the next two weeks, just until my sister comes back."

"Whatever you say." Mrs. Trykowski had been playing matchmaker for the better part of a year now, though Sean was having no part of it. "A ten," she repeated triumphantly. "She is the one, Sean. Remember this."

"I'm the one what?" Carly asked, looking a little unnerved.

Sean knew the feeling. Yes, Carly was smart and funny. Yes, there was something about her, but he'd known her all of a few hours. And anyway, no woman was ever going to be the one, not ever again. "Carly, this is Mrs. Trykowski. She lives next door and has clearly forgotten to take her medicine."

Mrs. Trykowski grinned.

Sean ushered her to the door. "They'll be hauling you away in a white jacket if you're not more careful."

Carly looked horrified.

Mrs. Trykowski laughed.

Melissa came down the hall doing the pee-pee dance. "Gotta go again, Uncle Sean!"

Sean could only groan, wondering what had happened to his nice quiet life.

3

IT WAS NOTHING short of a miracle, but finally, after needing water, a multitude of stories, three bathroom stops, monster checks in the closet and countless hugs good-night, Melissa was ready for bed.

As they had before, the hugs had stopped Carlyne cold. Her family never hugged good-night. In fact, they never hugged at all, but Melissa hadn't cared about Carlyne's reserve, she'd just crawled in her lap, wrapped her thin, bony arms tightly around Carlyne's neck and squeezed so tight Carlyne could hardly breathe.

"One more hug," the little girl pleaded. "Please?"

Carlyne had something sticky in her hair, grimy handprints all over her, and she couldn't wait to take a shower, but Melissa wouldn't let go.

"I miss my mommy," she whispered.

Carlyne's heart melted, and she found

herself stroking Melissa's hair. "I know, baby."

"You smell pretty." She burrowed her face into Carlyne's neck. "Like a mommy."

Startled by the unexpected lump in her throat, Carlyne held on.

"Night," Melissa finally said, kissing her cheek, leaving yet another sticky imprint.

Carlyne no longer cared. "Night," she whispered.

Exhausted, she practically had to crawl to her room, thinking if high-school students were forced to baby-sit, even for one afternoon, teenage pregnancy would vanish.

Unless good-night hugs were part of the package.

She was surprised that taking care of one little child could be more tiring than her social benefits and parties, but it definitely was. The thought of multiple children was terrifying.

And thrilling.

Sean's extra bedroom was much smaller than what she was used to. When she shut the door behind her, she was expecting to feel claustrophobic, but that didn't happen. The room was clean and simple, had a lovely glass sliding door, overlooking the back yard, and it felt...cozy.

Normally she reserved evenings for herself—when she wasn't attending one social event or another, that is. She craved quiet time, and she was ruthlessly selfish when she managed to steal it. She'd take long baths, walk or read.

Tonight was no different, though she had to admit, the need to get away from all the people around her didn't feel as strong as usual.

Still, she couldn't wait to strip down to the buff, to get out of the weight of the disguise of Carly. But instead, her feet took her to the sliding glass door, to the beautiful moonlit night beyond.

She'd been to many, many places, all across the world, but Santa Barbara was one of the most beautiful she'd ever seen. It was lush and green and fragrant, and in the distance, she could just hear the ocean, pounding the shore in relentless waves.

But far closer, in the pool just beyond the patio, swimming for all he was worth, was Sean.

She stepped out of the room and off the patio into thick wet grass that made her want to take off the hideous boots she still wore so her toes could sink in. Before she could stop herself, she made her way to the very edge of the pool.

The night was clear, cool and fairly quiet, except for the sound of Sean's long, powerful arms and legs slicing effortlessly through the water.

One lap. Two. Ten.

And still she watched, fascinated.

She could see a flash of smooth, sleek back. A tough, muscled shoulder. A long, lean flank. She had no idea why she felt something deep within her react when there were plenty of gorgeous men in her life. Plenty.

Okay, maybe not plenty, mostly because whatever men there were in her world, rich and educated and a perfect catch—just ask her mother—all bored her.

She had a feeling nothing about Sean would bore any woman.

Not that she planned on finding out. No, she couldn't add a quickie affair to her current list of sins. An affair, no matter how suddenly tempting, wasn't on her list of things to do while in the real world.

Learning who she was and what she was made of…that was her plan.

Sean, oblivious to her standing there, continued to swim beneath the starlit night until finally he slowed, then stopped only inches from where she stood, his body strong and pulsing and gleaming in the moonlight.

He was startled to see her. Shoving back his wet hair, he held onto the side of the pool, his chest heaving from exertion. Water ran down his face, over his strong, firm jaw. There was a drop on his lower lip, which he licked off with his tongue.

"You swim like a fish," she said inanely, as if she wasn't wishing he'd pull himself out of the water and give her a view of his body.

"Swimming is a stress reliever."

"Is there a lot of stress in your life, Sean O'Mara?"

She had no idea why she asked, why the obvious probe into his life. She didn't want to know about him, didn't want to become friends, because then she would care. And if she cared, she'd have to feel badly about using him and Melissa, not to mention all the little untruths she'd told.

Sean didn't look any more thrilled than she at the idea of sharing. "Some," he said, then purposely changed the subject. "You're looking a little worse for wear. Why don't you try swimming and see if it works for you?"

"You mean...now?"

At her surprise, he grinned. "No, next week. Yes, now."

"No, thanks."

He shook his head, and water flew. A drop hit the glasses that were continuously slipping off her nose, but she couldn't remove them to dry the lenses or she'd risk exposing herself.

"Come in," he said.

"In the *water*?"

He laughed again, and before she could so much as breathe, he reached out with one very big, very wet, warm hand and grabbed her ankle.

He tugged playfully.

Panic replaced any amusement Carlyne might have felt. She *couldn't* get wet. She'd lose her wig, her glasses, her contacts. Her clothes would cling to her, maybe slip off, and then the truth would be evident. She'd reveal who she really was...and the jig would be up.

She'd have to go home, and though the day had been nothing short of the most work she'd ever done, she'd loved it.

Loved it.

She wasn't ready to go back, not yet. Please, not yet.

"Come on, Carly." His fingers stroked the skin above her ankle.

Never in her life would she have imagined that spot to be an erogenous zone, but suddenly she had visions of him touching her like that all over.

His knowing eyes watched as he continued to stroke her in what should have been a completely innocent way, but nothing about Sean O'Mara was innocent when he looked at her that way, as if she could be eaten up in one bite.

"Come in," he coaxed. "Swim off the stress." He tugged on her ankle again, the pressure of his fingers going right through her big, clunky boot. The tingle spread directly between her thighs.

"No!" she said, much harsher than she intended, shoving the slipping glasses up her nose, pressing her other hand to the top of her head in case he dislodged the wig.

Though he didn't let go, his hold gentled, and the teasing went out of his eyes. "You don't swim?"

She blinked at him, nearly laughing in relief as he unwittingly gave her the out she needed. "No," she said quickly, shocking herself. This lying was getting too easy.

"That's dangerous." But he let go of her

almost reluctantly, and she shivered with something that had nothing to do with the slight chill in the air.

"Your family never made sure you learned?"

"No."

"Where did you say you grew up?"

"I didn't."

He looked at her for a long moment while she waited for him to grill her. "I could teach you," he finally said.

The image of him doing just that, of his nearly nude body brushing hers in the water, his work-roughened hands all over her— "Bad idea," she said, her pulse rocketing.

"I'm a good teacher."

No doubt, with a low, husky voice like that, he could teach her anything. Everything. "*Really* bad idea."

He didn't pressure her, just nodded. Then patted the brick edging of the pool. "Sit down, then, put your feet in. At least get used to the water."

He thought she was afraid. He had no idea that Princess Carlyne Fortier was afraid of nothing. Nothing at all. Except for maybe deep, dark, piercing eyes, a voice smooth as

whiskey and hands that promised heaven.
"I don't think—"

"Oh, come on. The pool won't bite." His
beautiful mouth curved. "I won't, either.
Not unless I'm invited."

"I'm not inviting, just so you know."

"You're not even going to put your toes
in?"

"No, I—" But before she could draw another breath, he'd untied her boots and was
tugging at them. To keep her balance, she
was forced to sit, right there on the edge,
and it wasn't a graceful sit, either, trying to
keep her modesty and not get wet. She
didn't get wet, but as for her modesty, with
Sean lower, still in the water, God only
knew what kind of view of her underwear
he'd gotten.

Panicked, she pressed her skirt closer to
her body. He slid his hands over her feet,
pulling off first her boots, then her socks.

And then her feet were in the deliciously
heated water, brushing against Sean's even
warmer body, and she could hardly breathe.

He hadn't seen anything, she told herself.
His head was bent, concentrating on her
feet, but then he looked at her.

She'd never seen a look of such
pure...heat, certainly not directed at her,

and it was titillating, to say the least. For a moment, she couldn't breathe, couldn't blink, couldn't move, but finally she managed a weak smile. "This is nice."

He didn't respond. Around them, the air sizzled with tension, *sexual* tension, and even as she told herself to get a grip, she wished she'd been wearing something, *anything* other than serviceable white panties. Leopard print, maybe, or even a thong. Something outrageous. Something as sexy as Sean.

"Tomorrow night wear your bathing suit," he said. "You can get all the way in. I'll show you how easy it is to swim."

Of course, she couldn't. But the sheer honesty in his gaze brought a twinge of guilt she was beginning to hate.

This, while exciting, thrilling, even arousing, was wrong. Very wrong. Knowing that, she got to her feet as gracefully as she could, which wasn't very, and backed away. "I have to go."

His arms and chest and belly flexed as he pulled himself out of the pool. He wore dark blue swim trunks that fit him like a second skin, molding his contours, his...shape in a way that made cohesive thought a distant memory. "It didn't chime midnight," he said, teasing in the face of the panic he couldn't possibly understand. "And anyway, running will do you little good. I know where you live."

But he didn't, really. He couldn't. She needed to be in her room with the door locked. She needed to pull off the itchy wig, needed to dump the glasses and contact lenses, needed to haul off the too many layers of clothes and give herself a good hard look in the mirror to remind herself who she really was.

Princess Carlyne Fortier. On vacation from her life. On a mission to find herself.

"I'm sorry," she whispered and, grabbing her boots, turned and ran.

Unlike Cinderella, she didn't leave anything behind.

SEAN WOKE AT DAWN to find Melissa sprawled across his feet like an orphaned puppy, fast asleep.

So were his legs.

It was like a bad nightmare. He couldn't escape her. For a moment he lay there and debated with his conscience. Now that he'd checked out Carly's references and she'd been approved by both himself and Melissa, he wanted to get to his office. But he could only imagine the fit Melissa would pitch when she woke up and found him gone, even with Carly just down the hall.

He showered and dressed, making as much noise as possible, but when he was ready for work, Melissa was still asleep, totally at home, smack in the center of his bed with his pillow and all the blankets.

A bed hog in the making.

With a sigh, he scooped her up and headed down the hall. In front of Carly's door, he shifted the dead weight in his arms and knocked.

Melissa stirred and snaked her arms around his neck. "Back to bed," she commanded gruffly.

"I'm going to work," he said, awkwardly patting her back. "I'm bringing you to Carly. Carly?" he called through the door.

"Uh... Just a second." Her voice was oddly frantic. There was lots of rustling, and then a...thud? "Coming!"

Finally, she opened the door. She had her thick makeup on. Her glasses were askew on her nose, and her hair looked as if it had exploded around her head during the night.

She looked rushed, unnerved and...oddly adorable.

But definitely not thrilled to see him.

"I've got to get to my office," he said. "And Melissa here just woke up, so—"

Without a word, she took Melissa.

"I'll be back tonight—"

The bedroom door shut in his face.

"Okay then," he said to no one. "Bye." Feeling more relieved than he should, he made his escape and headed to his car. Driving to his office for the first time since his sister had dumped Melissa on him.

He felt a twinge of guilt thinking of Melissa that way, as if she was an unwanted piece of luggage, but work was...well, his life. And it felt good to get back to it.

The first person he saw was Nikki, his secretary. "Hi, honey, I'm home," he said, skipping into his office. Feeling great. Feeling alone and loving it.

Nikki glared at him, which assured him that everything was, indeed, back to normal.

By noon, he'd dug himself out of the piles of work on his desk. He made a note to raise Carly's salary for saving his life. He met with clients without having to excuse himself to help one little four-year-old in the bathroom, and he vowed to also give Carly a big, fat hug to go along with her big, fat raise.

And when he clinched the deal with Sam,

finally, after working on the plans forever, he decided Carly should have a kiss to go with that hug.

A friendly kiss, of course. Just a little thank-you-for-saving-my-life kiss.

And it had nothing to do with the fact she'd given him a peek at her panties. Much.

It had been an inadvertent peek, sure, but he'd enjoyed it all the same. From his vantage point in the pool, he'd gotten a front-and-center view of her plain white bikini panties, cut high on the thigh, with enough material to cover her mound, but that material had been rather sheer. It had been dark, too dark to tell, but he'd imagined them wet.

It had made him hard then.

Hell, he was hard now. All those layers of clothes, hiding the best set of legs on this side of the Rockies. Not to mention what lay above those legs.

Why did she hide herself behind thick makeup and horrible glasses? And all those clothes? He wished he knew.

No. No, he didn't. That would mean he was thinking of getting involved, and he wasn't. What his nanny thought or did was none of his business, as long as she took good care of Melissa and left him out of it.

Way out of it.

Invigorated by this reinforced decision, he engrossed himself in work and was deeply involved with a new design when there came a light rap at his door.

And then another.

And another.

A continuing series of knocks, never letting up.

Nikki wouldn't dare do that, nor would anyone in the building, which made Sean groan, because he only knew one person, one little person, one little *nightmare* person, who'd start knocking like that and not stop.

Melissa.

From the other side of the door came Carly's voice. "Stop. I'm sure he heard you."

"I heard you, all right," he said after he'd opened the door, torn between irritation at the interruption and a surge of pleasure he didn't want to analyze.

Carly stood there, huge glasses covering most of her face, her clothes baggy and shapeless as usual. "Hi."

White panties, came the unbidden thought. *Wet white panties.* He wished like hell he could get them out of his head.

She held Melissa, who wriggled and wriggled until she was set free.

"Uncle Sean!" Beaming from ear to ear,

Melissa threw herself at him, flung herself in the air, leaving him no choice but to catch her before she hurt herself. "I missed you!"

Suffering her exuberant and very wet kiss, he glanced at Carly. He had a million things to do, but his nanny had a look he distinctly recognized.

High-level stress.

"Come home with us now," Melissa demanded, cupping his face in her little hands, forcing him to stop looking at Carly and to look directly at her. "I want you to be with us."

"I can't. I have work." Work was good. Work was great. Work was what he wanted.

Carly smiled apologetically. The neat woman from her interview yesterday was gone. Her hair looked ravaged. Her clothes were wrinkled. And she seemed to be wearing a good part of Melissa's lunch. But most curious, was her barely subdued sense of...panic?

"Everything okay?" he asked.

"Yes. I'm sorry." Carly looked embarrassed. "We had a long day and—"

"We burned the toast," Melissa announced, helping herself to the jar of chocolate kisses on his desk.

"Breakfast," Carly murmured. "Didn't come out too good."

"Neither did lunch," Melissa added.

"We didn't burn it, at least." Carly gave a tight smile. "The cake collapsed, that's all."

"Yep. Calaps," Melissa told him, pleased to be in the know. "But don't worry, we had clean-up time. And then we made play dough from itch."

"Scratch," Carly corrected.

"Scratch. It stuck to the pot. Set off the fire alarm." Melissa sent Sean a chocolately smile. "Mrs. T called the fire department, and two big trucks came! So then we drove here." She grinned and spread chocolate on some of his papers. "Carly said we could."

"Quite the day," Sean murmured to Carly, who bit her lower lip and pressed her thick-rimmed glasses to her face.

"Yes," she agreed. "It's been a long one."

He might have commented further but caught sight of Melissa climbing on his desk. "Try to keep those chocolate fingers off the plans, okay?"

"Okay!" But she had to lean over them to grab more of the kisses, which meant at least two more handprints.

Sean gritted his teeth and rolled the plans up.

"I hope you don't mind us showing up," Carly said as Nikki came into the room to offer drinks. "But..."

But she was exhausted, that was clear. Sean took pity, because he knew better than anyone the kind of exhaustion Melissa could provoke. He'd been living it for days before Carly had showed up to save his life.

But he did have to wonder at his supposedly *experienced* nanny. She had a résumé and references he had checked out, yet she wasn't acting so experienced.

Still there were those huge blue eyes of hers, magnified by those glasses. "It's okay," he heard himself saying. "I don't mind visitors."

Nikki stopped short of opening a soda and gaped at him. "Since when?"

"I could use a break," he said raising his eyebrows in such a way as to tell his nosy assistant he was trying to spare Carly's feelings.

"You hate breaks," Nikki said.

At Sean's glare, she rolled her eyes and vanished.

"Sean? You sure?" asked Carly.

No, he wasn't sure at all, but she looked so...desperate. And that little doubt came back, just a little niggle of it, but it was enough to disturb him.

Who was she, really?

Very uneasy that maybe she hadn't been completely honest with him, he took a big mental step back. His ex hadn't been honest, and that had nearly destroyed him. Now he had Melissa to think about, though what else could he do? He had very carefully and thoroughly checked Carly's references.

It had to be his attraction to her that bothered him.

"Uh-oh," Melissa said suddenly from the corner. She'd punched too many buttons on the fax machine, and paper started spitting out of it.

While he and Carly went closer, Melissa backed away. She fed Sean's discarded sandwich to the computer through its disk drive.

It started to smoke.

The fire alarm went off.

"Not again!" cried Melissa, covering her ears.

"Dammit!" Sean roared brilliantly.

Nikki came racing in, took one look at the disaster zone and brought her hands to her mouth to cover her shocked laugh.

"I can fix it," Carly assured them, fanning

air in front of the smoke detector until it stopped. Then she bent to the disk drive, which was making a funny noise.

Melissa's bottom lip continued to quiver. Then she opened her mouth and let out a sharp, earsplitting wail.

Sean struggled with his temper, overcome with the urge to strangle his sister for putting him in this position in the first place. Melissa belonged with her mother, not with him.

And then there was his nanny, who at this very moment was bent over his computer, glasses slipping down her nose, her huge sweater nearly falling off her creamy shoulders as she worked on his computer.

What kind of a nanny knew how to fix computer hardware? And why was he fighting a very male, very base urge to lean close and suck on that shoulder?

He took a deep, dragging breath and looked at Melissa, who was still crying. "I'm sorry I yelled."

Eyes full, she blinked at him. A hiccup racked her belly.

"I'm *really* sorry," he added.

She studied him, then lifted her arms. "Hug."

"Melissa—" But she was already crawling up his body, forcing him to do as she'd demanded and hug her. In his arms, she felt little and defenseless. Sweet.

And he'd scared her.

He felt about two inches tall.

"Love you, Uncle Sean," she whispered, yawning widely, setting her head on his shoulder.

Sean's throat tightened. "Love you, too." *Make that one inch tall.*

But then Melissa lifted her head, clutched her stomach, turned a distinct shade of green and said, "Uh-oh."

"Uh-oh?"

"I don't feel good."

"Oh, dear." Carly looked over at them. "How many chocolates did you eat?"

"All of them." And then threw up all over him.

4

THAT NIGHT, Carlyne locked her bedroom door and sank to her bed with a grateful whimper before so much as removing her shoes.

She needed to take off the heavy, itchy wig, remove her colored contacts and strip down before she fell asleep, but she could hardly move.

Despite her utter failure today, despite her exhaustion, she felt...happy. The work was harder than anything she'd ever done, yet it exhilarated her to be stretching herself. *Trying* at something.

Baffled at that, and more than a little confused about why she wanted to work like this when she didn't have to, she rolled over and dove through her bag for her cell phone, which she'd turned off when Sean had hired her. She turned it on. It was late, but that was her fault. She'd let Melissa sample the homemade play dough that morning and then a million or so chocolate kisses at

Sean's office. Was it any wonder the poor child had gotten sick all over him?

Then again in his car on the way home?

And once more in the living room?

Sean had been pretty gracious about the whole thing, really. He hadn't yelled again, though she could tell he'd wanted to. Instead, he'd scooped up Melissa—careful to hold her at arms' length—and had assured her she was okay.

Melissa had taken one look at him and had listened. She'd calmed down. She'd even wanted to hug him again, but Sean had managed to avoid that without hurting her feelings.

Just watching the two of them, Carly had felt that strange tightening in her throat. They didn't seem to know the particulars of what their relationship entailed, especially Sean. But he'd never walk away.

Had she really compared him to the men in her family?

She'd been wrong, very wrong. Her parents had rarely been around, certainly not when she'd been sick. It was something she'd always ached for when she'd been hurting—warm, secure, loving arms. She'd rarely gotten them.

Melissa had no idea how lucky she was.

"Poor little rich girl," Carlyne berated herself, pushing away the melancholy memories. No one in their right mind would spare a moment of pity for her.

On her cell phone, she punched in the numbers she knew by heart. "Francesca," she said the moment her assistant answered groggily. "How are you?" she asked in their native French.

"How am I? Terrific. You, on the other hand, you have problems." Francesca never held back to spare Carlyne's feelings, which was the biggest reason they were so close. "In fact, let me list them for you. You've run away from home...."

"I did not." Carlyne glanced at her still-shut door and lowered her voice. Wouldn't do to get caught speaking French. "Look, we discussed this when I called you yesterday. I'm all grown up, Francine, so it's entirely different when I go away. I'm...on vacation," she said, unwilling to try to explain the mission she was on.

"Uh-huh. Vacation. Without any money, without a car, without—"

"Look, I didn't call for a lecture. I could have called *home* for that."

"Speaking of which, you might want to

actually try that. Your parents have called looking for you. So has your cousin."

"Yeah, only because they need me for something or another. It's not as if they miss me."

Francesca went quiet for a moment, and Carlyne winced at how pathetic she'd sounded. "I'm sorry. That didn't come out right."

"What's the matter? You sound different."

She *was* different. She was *Carly* here, not Carlyne.

"Carlyne? Your mother is worried about that banquet you're putting on for the international press."

Heaven forbid her mother would call just to say hello. "Tell her everything is done. I'll earn her thousands for all those charities." And she would. It was Carlyne's specialty, coaxing rich people to part with their money.

"And your grandfather—"

"Needs something, too, no doubt. Francesca. *Help.*"

"What do you need? A way to get home? I can come myself, or send—"

"No, I don't want to leave." Not yet. She'd wanted a break from her life. A glimpse at how everyone else lived. Well, she'd had more than a glimpse. No one knew her. No one treated her like glass. No one expected cool sophistication and smooth elegance. No one expected her to be anything or anyone other than Carly.

She wanted more of that.

"The help I need is different," Carlyne said. "Francesca, if your sister had a kid, and she went off and left you with that kid for a couple of weeks because she had a job, would you watch after it?"

"Of course," Francesca said immediately.

Of course. That simple. Unconditional love. No question, no hesitation. "I wouldn't have said 'of course,'" Carlyne admitted quietly. "A few days ago I would have spent however much money it took and shipped the kid off for full-time care. And I probably wouldn't have given it another thought."

"Well, you're not exactly experienced in matters of the heart," Francesca said gently. "But while we're on that, I think maybe it's time for you to come clean."

"Clean?"

"With Sean. Carlyne, we talked about this already, remember? When you had me get your references. We agreed Sean should know who you really are."

"No, you agreed and I yessed you."

"*Carlyne.*"

"Okay, yes, he should know." She sighed, lay back and stared at the ceiling of her perfect, cozy little bedroom. "I'm just not ready to tell him yet." She looked out the window into the night, saw the flash of someone swimming in the pool. A strong arm. A long, powerful leg. A smooth, muscled back.

Her stomach tightened. "Not quite yet," she said softly.

Beneath the shimmering moon, Sean executed a somersault turn at one end of the pool and continued swimming with even, powerful strokes. "I've got to go," she whispered.

"But—"

"I'll call you again."

"See that you do. I'm worried about you." Across the miles Francesca let out a sigh. "Think about it, Carlyne. Think about how he'll feel when he does find out, on his own."

Sean's arms propelled his body through the water. "He won't."

"Why? Because you're unrecognizable?" Francesca laughed. "You've been dodging the paparazzi since you could walk, Carlyne. It's only a matter of time before you mess up or he gets a clue. Then he'll know your little secret, and I don't see him being happy at being made a fool, no matter what your intentions."

"It won't matter to him."

"It won't matter that he has a princess baby-sitting for him?"

"That title is nothing but froth."

"But it is your title."

In the water, Sean slowed slightly, his only sign of tiring. He'd finish soon and haul that leanly muscled body out of the water.

Carlyne wanted to watch. She wanted to be front and center. She didn't want to think about what would happen if he discovered her true identity. "I've got to go, Francesca."

"Just think about it, okay?"

"I will."

"Call me every day."

"I will. Bye." Instead of pulling off her disguise, as she'd been waiting all day to do, Carlyne opened her door and let in the cool, California night air.

Then she walked toward the pool.

When she was on the edge, she sat, careful to tuck her skirt beneath her this time so Sean couldn't reach for a leg and pull her in. But the memory of him doing just that the night before, of his large, still damp hand sliding up her ankle to grip her calf, altered her breathing.

He stopped swimming. Treading water in the middle of the pool, he looked at her with an intense but unreadable expression.

"Hey," she said softly.

"Where's your bathing suit?"

No greeting. No recriminations for destroying his office. Just where's your bathing suit. Her breathing quickened all the more because she could only imagine what would happen beneath the starless night sky if she'd put it on.

If she was really Carly.

But if she followed through with this crazy attraction, he'd discover the truth about her. Never again would he look at her the same. She knew this for a fact, because in her life, it had happened over and over again.

She had two kinds of acquaintances. The people who wanted to know her simply because of who she was and the kind who, once they found out, were too full of awe and disbelief to maintain any honest relationship at all.

That would happen here, too, and at the thought, her heart ached.

Caught by her own trap. Her own doing.

How had this happened?

This was supposed to be an escape. A little interlude in her life.

Only now she realized how others would be affected. Melissa.

Sean.

"Carly?"

God, that name. It represented all she wanted to be, open and free to do as she pleased. The opposite of Princess Carlyne Fortier, a woman tied by the bonds of responsibility and duty. "I didn't bring a bathing suit."

An odd mix of disappointment and relief crossed his face. "We could buy you one." He put two hands on the edge of the pool and with a flex of muscles that stole her breath, effortlessly pulled himself out of the water. Wet skin glimmered in the pale moonlight, and from the erotic position of sitting at his feet, she watched drop after drop run down the length of his body.

And what a body it was.

"Carly?"

She realized he'd said her name at least twice, and that he held out a hand.

Slipping hers in his, she let him pull her to her feet.

"About today," he said quietly, not letting

go of her hand, his intense gaze holding hers prisoner. "You seemed to be having a little trouble handling Melissa."

Oh, God, he *had* noticed. "I'm sorry about your office," she said.

"It survived."

Barely. "Yeah. Nikki is great, you know. She helped me clean up." Carlyne grimaced. "And then asked me not to visit you at work anymore."

"Sounds like Nikki." He grabbed his towel and started to dry off. "So...what happened?"

"It's new to me, Melissa's age." Sidetracked, she watched him dry his chest, his legs. "She's...very active."

He went still. "Too active?"

"No. No, I can do this. I know I can."

He straightened and tossed the towel aside. "Melissa said so, too. She said you're nice. The highest compliment, really, as she doesn't like many people these days."

He'd asked Melissa about her. Was it because he worried he'd made a hasty decision? Or was Carlyne unconsciously transmitting her own doubts?

"One thing I keep wondering about." He stepped a little closer. "You know computers. You were able to put mine back together with nothing more than a screwdriver and your wits."

Another degree and another special talent of hers. But it wasn't a passion, and it bored her.

"So how does a nanny know so much about hardware?"

"Oh, I picked up a little here and there."

There was a stray strand of hair in her face. Not her hair, it was the wig, but Sean reached out and touched it, tucked it behind her ear.

Too close, she thought with a hitch in her breath that had everything to do with his nearness, and she backed up a step.

His hand, still hovering, abruptly dropped to his side. "I'm sorry," he said quietly. "I shouldn't have done that, shouldn't have touched you."

"It's okay." *Do it again. Kiss me.*

His eyes smoldered. "What?"

Oh God, she'd spoken out loud, but before she could say a word—and really, what could she say when she'd spoken the utter truth—Sean let out a rough laugh. "I must be crazy to give you a chance to change your mind." He slipped a hand around her waist, his fingers stroking low on her spine, urging her even closer. His other hand curved around her neck, his fingers playing with the sensitive skin at her nape.

And his mouth, his beautiful, sexy mouth slowly descended to hers in a kiss that instantly stole her breath. He was still wet, enough that when she pressed herself against his tough, hard body, she became wet, too.

His hands molded her damp clothing to her body as he slid them over her, touching her waist, her ribs, cupping her bottom so he could rock against her.

And all the while, he continued to kiss her, using his lips, his tongue, even his teeth, nibbling and sucking her to such a mindless state that she might have given herself away if he hadn't pulled back, breathing harshly.

"What else about you is going to be a surprise?" His mouth was wet from hers. His chest rose and fell with each ragged breath.

"N-nothing."

"I doubt that. All I know is what you had on your résumé, and what your references were able to tell me about your capabilities. Not much, really."

And all fabricated. Which meant he really knew nothing about her.

"Carly?"

That name again, and she winced before

she could stop herself. "I'm sorry," she whispered, willing him to understand. "I...don't like to talk about myself."

Something flickered in his eyes, something tense and uncertain, but then it was gone, and he sent her a tight smile. "Me, either."

An impasse. Good. And though it wasn't what she wanted, she bent for his towel, handed it to him and walked away.

SHE WOKE UP EARLY. Or more accurately, got out of bed early, as she hadn't slept much.

Sean was beginning to doubt her. Which meant she was definitely on borrowed time. But she wasn't ready to give it all up, not yet.

She donned the robe and slippers she'd purchased at her special store. The robe was terry cloth and itchy. The slippers, the only ones she could find in her size, had a bunny on each. "Classy," she said into the mirror.

Feeling very middle America, she walked outside to get the morning paper.

"Psst!"

Mrs. Trykowski, her dyed-red hair rolled in green curlers, her short, heavy body in a zebra-print, faux-silk robe, was waving wildly. "Yoo-hoo!" she cried, in a single bound leaping over the bushes that separated the yards. "Good morning, Carly!"

Startled, Carlyne dropped the paper.

"I'm so glad I caught you," Mrs. T said when she'd reached Carlyne. "I wanted to tell you...first of all, that dark hair just isn't you."

"But..."

"And second, the way to Sean's heart is through his stomach."

"*What?*"

"Catching Sean, dear," the older woman said patiently. "You do it through his stomach."

"Um...okay." Carlyne smiled through her teeth and backed toward the door, thinking, *Crazy lady alert.*

"You think I'm making this up. That's what others thought, too, and they all failed."

No, she wasn't going to ask.

"Go ahead, dear," Mrs. T said with a knowing smile. "Ask. I know you're dying to."

In the end, Carlyne couldn't help herself. "Others?"

"Well, he's a handsome man, don't you think?"

Gorgeous. But absolutely beside the point. "How many others?"

"Oh, I really couldn't tell all his secrets," she said demurely. "Just trust me. Feed him. Cook for him. It'll work."

This was insane. "I'm not looking for his heart."

"Well, now. There's no reason to lie." And with another knowing smile, the woman waddled away.

Carlyne shook her head and went inside, through the kitchen, where she stopped and stared at the stove.

The way to his heart is through his stomach.

Well, Carlyne didn't want his heart, though his body would be nice.

And yet she *was* rather hungry. But where to start?

Until she'd come here, she'd never done more than boil water or push the buttons on the microwave. She'd never seen her own mother in a kitchen, other than to thank the chef.

But really, how hard could it be? She was a college graduate, for God's sake. She could do this. After rolling up her sleeves, she cracked some eggs and dropped them in a pan, contemplating the stove for a moment before turning on the burner. Eggs, no problem. She shoved bread into the toaster. Easy enough. Then she threw some sausage in another pan and flicked on that burner, too. Pancakes took some extra doing, as she had to open the one and only cookbook she found, but following a recipe was easy. Any idiot could do that, right?

So why was the batter thick and sticky enough to form sidewalks?

She was contemplating that when the eggs started making an unusual popping sound—or maybe not unusual, she really had no idea. But when she tried to stir the boiling mess, it was…rubber.

Probably not good. Then she smelled smoke.

Oops. The toaster was on fire. Definitely not good. With a little screech, she snatched it away from the paper-towel rack, pulled the cord from the wall in the process, then promptly dropped it to the floor.

"Ouch!" There was a smoldering toaster at her feet, and the eggs were still popping, probably close to igniting, too. She was a complete and utter failure at being normal, and oh, my God, she'd set her bunny slippers on fire when she'd dropped the toaster.

That was it, the final straw, and the princess who never cried burst into tears. Then suddenly a big, tough, strong body sat her down on the floor and was slapping at the flaming bunny heads.

While she sat there staring at the burned fuzz, sniffling, overwhelmed by a bad case of self-pity, Sean efficiently and quickly smothered the small flame still coming out of the toaster.

He reached up and turned off the stove.

Then—and this was the part she'd never forget—he dropped to his knees, scooped her against that chest that was even more magnificent up close and personal, and peered into her face.

"You okay?" he demanded hoarsely. "Are you hurt?"

He had the most amazing eyes. And those hands...hands that were at this very moment running over her body, looking for burns, she supposed.

"Carly?"

Oh, my, he felt good. *She* felt good.

"Carly!"

He'd plastered her against him so they had full body contact, which was fabulous as all he wore was jeans—unfastened. And okay, yes, it had been *way* too long since she'd felt such delicious contact, but it wasn't the lack of sex in her life that was making her dizzy.

It was Sean.

"Carly! Talk to me!"

His rough, edgy voice was like a bucket of cold water. While she'd been melting into a little pool of longing, he was anxious and probably furious. He certainly wasn't helplessly turned on, not as she was, and why would he be? She wasn't a glamorous princess, but a normal plain Jane. This man could have any woman he wanted— why would he want her? "I'm..." *Pathetic.* "...fine."

Not satisfied, he reached for her hair, probably to smooth it out of her face, and she catapulted into action, because what if he dislodged the wig? Leaping to her feet, she grabbed for a kitchen towel. "Don't worry, I've got everything completely under control now."

"Carly—"

"We're lucky I wore out the batteries on your smoke detectors yesterday." She bustled around, tossing dirty pans into the sink, avoiding his gaze. "I promise, I'm not in the habit of setting the kitchen on fire every time I make breakfast."

Mostly because she'd never made breakfast before.

Darn it, this was all Mrs. Trykowski's fault.

Rising to his feet, Sean glanced at the flat, lumpy pancakes. Then at the burned-to-a-crisp sausages and rubber eggs. He raised an eyebrow. "Do this a lot, do you?"

"Sure." Another pan hit the sink. It would probably never come clean, not with her expertise, anyway. "Every morning."

"Really?" His expression changed, went guarded. It was as if he just…vanished. He was standing right there in front of her, yet he was gone. Eyes flat, mouth grim, gone. "And you're not hurt?" he asked in a polite voice twenty-five degrees cooler than he'd been only a second ago.

"No. Sean…"

He avoided her gaze. "As you've mentioned, cooking isn't in your job description. I'll handle it from now on."

"But—"

No buts. He'd recognized the lie, was probably disgusted. He walked out the door.

5

SEAN TRIED to immerse himself in work. It should have been easy.

But he couldn't concentrate. It had never happened to him before, this blankness when it came to designing. Yet every job he looked at, every file, every single blueprint faded away, leaving him instead with the image of Carly when he'd walked out of the kitchen yesterday morning.

She'd been trying to make them breakfast. Why, he had no idea. It was painfully obvious she didn't have a clue. And it was equally, painfully obvious he had a problem.

First, he'd lost more than a few brain cells when he'd pulled her against his chest, but the embrace had been driven by a real fear that she'd burned herself. Instead, *he* felt scorched. The sweet scent of her, the softness of her skin…the catch of her breath.

It all reminded him of how he'd felt when they'd kissed. Whole. He'd felt whole.

But then he'd watched her luscious lips form the words "every morning" to his question of how often she cooked, and he'd heard the lie. He'd heard it, he'd seen it, he'd felt it.

And he'd lost it. That simple.

Tina again, of course. Still torturing him with memories. Well, dammit, he was over her. Over and moved on.

But damn if he'd trust anyone in the near future or let a woman ever hurt him again.

He finally got into his work, but for the first time in his life, he had to force himself. All he could think about was how the house was faring. He hoped it wasn't on fire or destroyed. He hoped everyone was in one piece.

He hoped…ah, hell. He was full of it. He wanted to see Melissa. He wanted to see Carly.

But by the time he got home, it was yet again very late. Too late. The house was still standing, thank God, but quiet. No Melissa. No Carly. They were both asleep.

Well, good. This was what he'd wanted. Peace and quiet. Yep. Perfect.

To prove it to himself, he worked like a fiend for several more days, without taking a breather, with no more than a quick check on Melissa, who was apparently thriving. As promised, he made sure to leave an easy breakfast waiting for them and something for dinner, as well, or money for take-out.

While he was doing all that, he couldn't shake the new and entirely unwelcome feeling that work was keeping him from something important.

From something like…his life.

CARLYNE COULDN'T believe it. Sean managed to avoid her for days. This was a new experience, being avoided, ignored, and she didn't like it.

But this was *his* world. He could defy her, ignore her, fire her. Anything. He was in charge, which was yet another new and unwelcome realization for a woman who had been wrapping people around her pinky finger since before she could even walk.

"I wanna swim," Melissa said to her one afternoon in the second week.

Carlyne looked at the little girl, who'd stripped out of her clothes and was standing there naked as the day she was born, an angelic smile on her face. "How about a bath?"

"No bath," Melissa said firmly. "Pool."

"No pool. Bath."

"No."

"Yes."

"*No*," Melissa said in a whine.

"No," Carly repeated after the petulant girl.

"Yes." Melissa stopped short, then frowned. "*Hey!*"

Carlyne had no intention of getting in the water. Too dangerous. Sean had been gone every day, all day, in fact, but she couldn't bank on it. With Sean, she could bank on nothing.

"But I swim good!" Melissa insisted, her chin jutting stubbornly into the air.

Well, actually, that made two of them. At home Carlyne had a case of gold medals and trophies. Big whoop-de-do. "Go get clean clothes, I'll start the tub."

Melissa just sent her that same angelic smile, which upon reflection should have been Carlyne's warning. But happily clueless, she went into the bathroom to start the water.

The little girl didn't appear. "Melissa?" She wasn't in her bedroom. Or the kitchen. Or the living room.

"Oh, my God!" At a full run, Carlyne hit the back yard, and sure enough, there was that little blond head bobbing in the pool. Without another thought, Carlyne dove in.

By the time she reached Melissa, her heart was pumping so loud she couldn't hear a thing over the roar of her blood. Scooping the little girl up, she clutched her close to her chest and swam for the side.

Melissa grinned. "See? Told you I could swim." Struggling out of Carlyne's arms, she slipped out of the pool and danced excitedly on the concrete. "I could have stayed under longer, but you swim fast."

Carlyne, champion swimmer, could hardly pull herself out of the water because her knees were shaking so violently.

"Why is your hair crooked?" Melissa asked, staring at her with fascination. "And your face...it's melting." She tipped her head to the side. "How come?"

Because she had on thick foundation, which felt like papier-mâché on her skin. She dragged herself up, held her wig on her head with one hand and pointed toward the house. "Go."

"But—"

"Go. Dry. Off."

At the unaccustomed sharpness of Carly's voice, Melissa blinked in stunned surprise. Then, predictably, her bottom lip started the quiver. "You mad at me?"

Carlyne sighed. She'd lost her glasses in

the pool. She'd have to go after them. Her clothes were clinging to her body, and if she wasn't mistaken, one contact lens had slipped. But none of this was Melissa's fault. She certainly hadn't asked for her mother to leave the country or to be left with a commitment-challenged uncle. Or stuck in the care of a runaway princess pretending to be a nanny.

Melissa's eyes filled. "Sorry."

"Oh, honey." Carlyne sagged with exhaustion. "*I'm* sorry. It's just that you scared me. Now we need to get all dried and changed because your uncle Sean might be home soon."

Not that he'd been home before ten o'clock at night all week, but that wasn't Melissa's fault, either.

Turning to usher Melissa in the house, she stopped short.

Over the fence appeared Mrs. Trykowski's face. She was clearly standing on something, clinging to the wood, watching them. Spying. When she saw Carlyne's horrified expression, the woman smiled and waved. "Hellooo!"

Carlyne held her wig and tried not to think about the makeup running in rivulets down her face. Had that been an I-know-who-you-are hello? Or a hey-I-just-love-to-spy-on-my-neighbor wave?

God only knew.

Heart in her throat, Carlyne managed a weak wave and vanished into the house, certain her cover was blown.

No matter. Her two weeks were nearly up, anyway. She'd known it would have to end.

She just hadn't known how very much she wouldn't want it to.

NOBODY WAS MORE surprised than Sean when Mrs. Trykowski called him at the office. He transferred the woman to the speakerphone because he and Nikki were hands deep in the piles behind his desk, looking for a missing blueprint.

"Just wanted to tell you everything is going great at the house," Mrs. Trykowski said, as if she called him every day to check in.

Sean exchanged a puzzled look with Nikki and let out a little laugh. "Good. Okay. Well…thank you."

"Aren't you going to ask me details?"

"Details?"

"Sure, as in what Melissa is up to."

"Well…"

"And let's not forget your live-in."

"The nanny," Sean corrected.

"Whatever you kids call it these days," she said with a secret smile in her voice.

Nikki looked at Sean speculatively.

Sean shook his head. "Listen, Mrs. Trykowski, I'm really busy here, and—"

"They're having a ball, you know. Laughing, giggling, playing... So, when are you going to marry her?"

"Marry—" He nearly choked. "Now just back the truck up."

Nikki, familiar with Sean's past and his lack of inclination to go for another relationship, grinned widely.

"She's really just the nanny," Sean said weakly.

"Uh-huh," Mrs. Trykowski said kindly. "And I just had mind-blowing, head-banging, screaming sex last night."

"Mrs. Trykowski!"

"Well, honestly, Sean O'Mara. That woman you have in your house, she's the one to make it shine for you, she could fill it with love and laughter—"

And fire, Sean thought darkly. *Let's not forget the fire.*

"That woman could really turn your place into a home. She's no simple nanny, and you know it. Now what I want to know is, what are you going to do about it?"

"Well, I—"

"Oh for heaven's sake." A disgusted sigh came over the line. "Don't tell me you're going to be a male about this. Figures." Another loud huff of breath. "Then don't ask me to tell you what they're up to again, you big, silly fool." And she hung up on him.

"I didn't ask you in the first place," he muttered.

"Interesting." Nikki was looking at him in a new light. "You and the nanny, huh?"

"Stop it." But he had to admit, Mrs. T had spiked his curiosity. What were they doing? "Look, I'm going," he said, picking up his keys.

Nikki's mouth fell open. "As in…going to your house?"

"Where else?"

"But it's the middle of the day."

"Yep." He grabbed his briefcase, then stopped, looking at it. "No work tonight," he decided, tossing it onto his desk.

"You've never left in the middle of the day before." She watched him walk to the door. "Don't forget to invite me to the wedding."

WHEN HE ARRIVED, the house was silent. His heart started a funny, heavy pounding as he moved through the living room toward the definitely empty kitchen.

Where were they?

Granted, he hadn't been around much. Okay, not at all, but they had to be here. Panicked, he ran. "Melissa! Carly!"

Then, in the hallway, he suddenly heard it. Laughter. They were outside, in the back yard, sitting under the shade of a large elm tree, both looking happy and content.

The sun hit Carly's dark hair and her thick glasses, which nearly blinded him with the glare. Her heavy makeup was firmly in place. And those clothes...she wore a ton of them. A long, shapeless, flowery sundress, a sweater, her usual boots. No skin showed beneath her chin.

It didn't matter.

The feel of her warm, lush curves, the taste of her sweet, sexy mouth were permanently imprinted on his brain.

He couldn't take his eyes off her. He didn't understand that. She wasn't beautiful, not by a long shot. But when she smiled at Melissa, her entire face lit up.

And Sean's heart took a tumble.

Melissa had something smeared across

her face, and even as he watched, she shoved what looked like a cookie in her mouth, leaving even more of a mess on her face. "Yum," she said around a mouthful.

"Well, you can thank yourself," Carly told her with a smile. "You did all the mixing."

"No fire," Melissa said with obvious glee.

"No fire," Carly agreed dryly. "I've stayed clear of the toaster, thank you very much."

"Uncle Sean!" Melissa cried, catching sight of him.

The little pixie rose to her feet, shoved the last of her cookie in her mouth and sprinted for him.

By now, Sean knew what was coming. He spared a thought for the shirt he wore. His favorite. He thought of the chocolate that was going to hit it and probably stain it, and with a resigned sigh, he opened his arms.

She leaped right into them with such faith he found his arms tightening around her in a hug he hadn't known he needed to give.

"Nice day?" he asked her, burying his face in her sun-warmed hair because she smelled like summer, like cookies, like one-hundred-percent kid.

Nodding, she did her best to smear chocolate all over him. "We made cookies, but we were real careful, Uncle Sean. No fire."

Sean glanced over her head and met Carly's eyes. She wasn't smiling, just watching him. He watched her back.

"And then we walked around the block," Melissa continued happily. "We laughed at Mrs. Trykowski's cat cuz she chased a squirrel up a tree and got scared. And stuck. Then I was hot. Really hot, Uncle Sean, so that's why I did it. That's why I went swimming."

Sean's heart stopped. "Swimming?"

"Uh-huh. Water's warm."

Hard to talk when there sat a lump in his throat the size of a regulation football. "You aren't supposed to go in the pool without me, Melissa. Remember?"

Melissa lifted her head, looking both contrite and thrilled at the same time. "I remember. But I forgot. And I scared Carly and she jumped in."

Sean stared at Carly. "But she doesn't know how to swim."

"Oh, yes, she does," Melissa told him. "She swam right to me, really fast. Then when I told her I could swim, she cried *and* laughed. Right, Carly?"

Carly swallowed hard, her gaze never leaving Sean's. "Right, Melissa."

Slowly, because his heart was still thundering in his ears, Sean set Melissa down and continued to stare at Carly. "You told me you couldn't swim."

"I know."

She knew. Damn, but he'd done it again, fallen sucker to another woman who lied. "Melissa, why don't you go pick out some stories for me to read to you?"

"But you always say you're too busy to read to me."

He winced. What kind of an uncle was he that he hadn't made any time for his niece? "I'm sorry about that. I was wrong. Go pick a few out. Take your time."

Melissa clapped, then skipped to the house.

Carly rose, probably hoping to escape, as well.

"Wait," he said.

She looked toward the house. "I thought I should help her—"

"She's fine."

"Then I should—"

"Stay," he said, putting a hand on her arm. An electric current seemed to run through them, and annoyed that now, even now, she could still get to him, he dropped his hand.

She crossed her arms and stepped back.

A defensive pose. Sean's heart twisted. "Let's get this straight, okay?"

"Okay."

"You can't cook, though you said you could. But you *can* swim, though you said you couldn't."

"Yes." Her voice was a mere whisper, and she was studying the tops of her boots, apparently fascinated.

"Carly…" He let out a disparaging sound, struggling with temper, wanting even now to give her a chance to explain herself.

She didn't take it.

"Is there something wrong?" he prompted, willing her to give him something, anything. "Are you in some kind of trouble?"

"No!"

Too fast, he thought with a surge of worry.

"What, then? What do I need to know that you haven't told me?"

"Nothing."

Frustrated, he turned away, staring blindly at the pool, thinking he should let it go. But he couldn't seem to do that. After Tina, he'd started swimming laps to relieve stress.

Suddenly, he had a whole lot more stress

to relieve. "I can't do this again," he said grimly.

"What?"

"Never mind." He wasn't about to admit he'd been this stupid twice in his life. "Look, you don't want to trust me, fine. But I'm trusting you with Melissa, and I'd like more references. Can you do that?"

She swallowed hard, her only sign she'd heard him. "Yes."

Heart heavy, he headed inside.

"Sean?" she called, making him stop and look at her. "I'd never hurt Melissa."

"I know."

"Can I stay? For the few days there are left?"

Her eyes were eager. Hopeful. And dammit, that made him ache. "You can stay," he said quietly, wondering why her relieved smile reached him when he didn't want to be reached, not by her.

6

SHE WASN'T a princess in disguise, she was a chicken.

Late last night, long after Melissa had fallen asleep and Sean's light had finally gone off, long after Carlyne had snorted in disgust over the television news, which was still claiming she was either in a hospital suffering exhaustion or on an extravagant vacation in the Bahamas, she'd slipped a sheet of paper beneath Sean's bedroom door.

More references. That they were newly manufactured by Francesca didn't make Carlyne feel any better. Nor did the fact that she still hadn't told him the truth about herself.

She couldn't tell him, not yet.

Francesca was mad at her. Sean was mad at her.

And she was mad at herself.

Not to mention nervous. Sean had left her a message on the machine saying he'd be home in time to take Melissa out for a burger, which the little girl had been asking him to do for several days.

Carlyne was sure she wasn't included in the invitation, so she sat on the porch watching Melissa play in the grass, waiting for Sean.

When she heard a rustle in the tree by the fence, she rose to her feet with a sense of resignation. Melissa was still happily playing on the far side of the yard, oblivious, so Carlyne didn't bother to lower her voice. "Mrs. Trykowski?"

The rustling in the tree grew louder. There came a muffled curse.

"I know you're up there." She had to face this. She'd hadn't slept a wink since she'd gone for that inadvertent swim. If Mrs. Trykowski had recognized her, Carlyne needed to know. "You're going to hurt yourself."

"Oh, no, dear. I'm an expert tree climber."

The branches wriggled wildly as the old woman let herself be seen. "I've been climbing this tree for a long time now."

"What? Why?"

Though the tree was on Mrs. Trykowski's side of the fence, the woman swung down from a branch and dropped to the ground on Sean's side. "Why?" the older woman asked incredibly. "So I know what's going on, of course."

"Don't you think if people wanted you to know, they'd tell you?"

"Well, you'd think so, wouldn't you?" Sniffing, she straightened her plaid cotton housedress. Her knee-high stockings had fallen to her ankles, and she had a twig in her hair. "But not Sean. He keeps his emotions right next to his closed-off heart, where they're safe."

"Closed-off heart?"

"You know about his ex."

No. No, she didn't.

"A horrible woman, Tina was. Well, actually, she was one of those incredibly beautiful women, a homecoming queen, if I'm not mistaken. But she couldn't tell the truth to save her life. They were going to get married, but she lied about everything—her shopping bills, where she'd been, what she'd been doing, her hair..."

"Her hair?" Carly asked weakly, touching the ends of her wig.

"She pretended to be a natural blonde." Mrs. Trykowski's eyes were sharp. "No one is born *that* blond, honey. The point is, she broke his heart but good. I am very glad you plan on mending it."

"Oh, but—"

"Just don't ever lie to him."

Carlyne looked into Mrs. Trykowski's sky-blue, guileless eyes and searched for answers. Did she know?

Impossible to tell.

The older woman tipped her head to the side, as if considering the matter, and Carlyne held her breath.

"Please don't betray him. I'd really hate to see that. He wouldn't like to think so, but he could still be easily hurt. Especially by a woman he cares about."

"I—I don't intend to hurt him." *Don't you?* taunted a small voice.

"Melissa is doing so well," Mrs. T said.

Carlyne turned her head and found Melissa walking toward them, a big, warm grin on her face. The grin was for Carly, and she found herself returning it. And just that simply, Carlyne's heart tripped. Or maybe not just that simply, at all.

Truth was, she was completely, hopelessly in love with the little girl. She hadn't counted on that.

It was supposed to be temporary.

So what was this serious longing pulsing through her? A longing for a husband and a precious child of her own? And an even more secret longing…that her family could be as wonderful as Sean and Melissa.

When Sean's car drove up, Carlyne fought the urge to run to him and tell him everything. But it was too late for that. Far too late.

Melissa went racing toward him, bounding into his arms, which he'd opened for her. He settled her into her car seat, then turned and sought out Carlyne.

As Carly.

Carlyne suddenly couldn't tell the difference between the two personas. Which one *was* she?

Carlyne?

Carly?

Who did she *want* to be?

Across the yard, their gazes met. Hers was hesitant, but his wasn't. He looked sure and confident, and he was smiling.

Carly, she thought. Definitely, she wanted to be Carly.

"See that?" Mrs. Trykowski whispered in her ear. "He's thinking impure thoughts about you right this very second."

"Mrs. Trykowski!"

"Well, he is. Don't waste them now, you hear?"

If anyone was thinking impure thoughts,

it was Carlyne as Sean came toward her. He was fully dressed, of course, but she could see him as he looked at night, getting out of his pool, wearing only wet trunks clinging to his hard, toned body.

"Coming?" he asked.

"Well, I—" She forced the image of his sleek, drenched body out of her head. "I don't— You and Melissa—" Sighing, she shut her mouth. Since when wasn't her delivery smooth and articulate? She'd spoken in front of hundreds of people at a time. She'd been keeping her cool since she could walk.

But somehow, Sean O'Mara threatened her entire facade with a look.

"Aren't you hungry?" he asked.

The question seemed loaded, but his eyes were dark, unreadable. He wore his office attire. Khakis and a polo shirt. Simple clothes, but not a simple man. Intelligence blared from his eyes and expression. His body was tenser than he'd let on, and beneath the smooth cotton of his shirt, every muscle was delineated and defined.

Trouble. He was trouble personified. At least in terms of her mental health.

"I don't know," she said.

"Get in the car, Carly."

Surprised at herself, she did. When he'd driven away from the curb, she asked, "Did you call my new references?"

He looked at her, then turned his head and watched the road. His jaw was tight. "Yes."

"Did they check out?"

"Didn't you expect them to?"

He met her gaze again briefly, but this time she looked away first. "Yes. Sean..." She glanced at Melissa in the back seat. She was busy sucking on her fingers. Carlyne lowered her voice. "Despite the kitchen fiasco and the fact I don't really cook—"

He made a noise that sounded like a snort of agreement.

"Despite the fact that maybe I'm not your typical nanny, I really am a good caretaker for Melissa."

"We agreed on that fact last night, or you wouldn't still be here."

"So you do trust me that much, at least."

Again he flicked her a glance. "That much, yes. But I'd like to know more about you. You haven't volunteered an ounce of information."

"Neither have you."

He fell silent.

The radio wasn't on. Melissa was oddly

quiet. Which left Carlyne with nothing to distract her from the way Sean's long legs flexed every time he braked or clutched. His hand worked the gearshift with a natural ease that had her mind drifting to other things.

Such as what else he could do with those hands.

What he could do to a woman's body. To *her* body.

She was pretty desperate if her mind had wandered in that direction about this man. "How's work?" she asked, desperate for a diversion.

"Busy."

"Nikki good?"

"Yep."

"What are you working on?"

"Work."

Subject clearly closed. Well, too bad. She needed to talk before the silence killed her. "Busy with your designs?"

He lifted a surprised brow.

"I do know what an architect does."

"It's not the actual work I'm too busy with," he admitted. "I love that part. It's the other. The dealing with rich, spoiled clients. Soothing ruffled egos. Attending silly cocktail parties to promote my work."

"Parties?" They happened to be her forte, parties. Not that she missed wearing heels and stockings, but there was something to be said for the excitement of pulling it all together. "You have to go to a lot of them?"

"One in particular. This Saturday night," he added in a voice that told her he'd rather have an impacted wisdom tooth removed without novocaine.

"It isn't so bad, really," she told him. "Just hold a drink in your hand and keep moving. Oh, and keep smiling."

He flicked her an interested glance. "You sound like you know what you're doing."

"Well..."

"You can come with me, then."

"What?"

She didn't know who was more surprised. Sean, that he'd asked, or her. "But what about Melissa?" she asked. "She'll—"

"She'll be fine with Mrs. Trykowski for the night. Hey, it's your own fault," he said, sounding grumpy. "You looked interested. You can keep me in line."

Yes, but who would keep *her* in line?

They didn't talk again until they were seated in the noisy, bustling fast-food restaurant. They sat in front of the kiddie area, where Melissa had vanished. The small table was shaped like a hamburger. Their knees bumped. Their feet touched. And when they reached for their drinks at the same time, their hands brushed.

Overly sensitized to his touch, Carlyne drew back abruptly, knocking all her French fries to the floor.

"Here." Sean reached into his bag and grabbed a fry. He dipped it in ketchup and lifted it to her lips.

His eyes were full of challenge and something else entirely, something that made her skin feel itchy and hot.

He waved the fry beneath her nose. It smelled heavenly.

But then again, so did Sean. "Sean, what are you doing?"

"Feeding you."

"But—"

"Open."

"I don't think—"

"Open," he said again, touching her lower lip with the fry, dabbing a drop of ketchup there, which she sucked off. The little sucking noise seemed exorbitantly loud.

SEAN FELT that noise to the depth of his toes, but mostly right between his thighs. And when Carly sunk her teeth into the French fry, he nearly moaned. "Good?" he asked in a voice gone thick with unexpected desire.

"Yes, but—"

"Eat, Carly."

"But you don't even like me," she reminded him.

"I'm just feeding you." *Just looking at you. Just wanting you.*

She drew the rest of the fry into her mouth. When she licked the remaining salt off her lower lip, he tore his gaze from hers and watched her mouth. It was a fascinating mouth. Wet, with a little bit of ketchup right...

She made a sound when he touched her lips. And when he dragged his finger across her lower lip, she made that sound again, an almost helplessly aroused noise that came from deep in the back of her throat.

"You have some..." His finger made the pass again, and when her tongue darted out to hit the spot, finger and tongue collided.

He let out a rough groan. "Carly—"

Her eyes closed as if the name somehow bothered her, but that was silly, it was her name, and then her tongue touched his finger again and he had to stop thinking because he lost all the blood in his head for parts south.

"You missed it," he whispered hoarsely, and he bent forward, still holding her gaze until the last possible second, until their lips were nearly touching, until her long lashes drifted down, hiding her expression.

Until they were kissing.

Softly. Tentatively. Sweetly. And then that gentle connection wasn't enough. Sean pulled back and reached for her glasses. He wanted them off, wanted no barriers.

"No, I want to see this," Carly protested, her hands coming up, holding the glasses on.

He wasn't going to argue. Cupping her face, Sean shifted closer and—

Nothing.

Because there came a tug on his shirt. "Can I have ice cream now, Uncle Sean? I been good. Really, really, really good."

Melissa stood there, her eyes big and intent on her mission.

Carly's eyes were big, too, and they landed on him with the same question he had. How long had Melissa been standing there?

Had she seen that impromptu—and totally inappropriate—kiss? And how had it happened? One moment he was teasing her with that French fry and the next...

"Aren't you done talking yet?" Melissa wanted to know.

"Yes." Carly surged to her feet. Careful to avoid Sean's gaze, she grabbed Melissa's hand. Her breathing wasn't quite even, the only hint of any inner turmoil. "Let's get that ice cream, kiddo."

7

SHE WASN'T GOING to be able to sleep, so she didn't even try. Instead, Carlyne slipped out of her bedroom through the sliding glass door.

The back yard was silent. The pool empty.

With a little sigh, she stretched out on a lounge chair, put her hands beneath her head, tipped up her chin and studied the sky.

"Not tired?"

Sean. He was sitting in the lounge chair right next to her, in the shadows, and she'd been so intent on the fact he hadn't been swimming, she hadn't even noticed him right beside her. She noticed him now, noticed every inch of his long, powerful legs, his gleaming broad shoulders. And that flat, hard belly...she could never get enough of looking at it.

Then that belly tightened as he coiled, straightened and came to her side.

"I was just thinking about you," she whispered.

"About how we kissed?"

Trust him to be so blunt. "Yes."

"What about it?"

"Well, it was…good, for one."

His mouth curved.

"And now I can't stop thinking about it."

Slowly, his eyes dark and solemn, he sat again—on her lounge. Their hips bumped, and when her glasses slipped, he reached out and fixed them with a gentle finger. "What else are you thinking about? For once, Carly, tell me what's going on inside you. It's not all about just a kiss."

"That was just a kiss?" She sat up, feeling exposed laying there beside him, but he leaned close with a hand on either side of her hips.

"It was more than just a kiss, I'll give you that," he said quietly. "But what else, Carly? What else goes on inside that head of yours? I can't stop wondering about you. Who you are, where you came from."

"It's…not that important."

"Like hell. I can't stop thinking about you, and then there's how you make me feel when we kiss." To show her, he did just that, leaned forward and put his mouth to hers.

She felt it all the way to her toes and back up again. She felt it in every erogenous zone in her body.

And she felt it to the bottom of her heart, which brought her back to her problem.

At the restaurant, Sean had sunk his fingers into her hair, but it hadn't been *her* hair, it had been the wig. One more second and he would have dislodged it, ruining her disguise and destroying any feelings he had toward her.

It could happen again, right now. He'd learn the truth and it would be all over.

Ironic, since in the beginning, she'd wanted only to immerse herself in the Carly persona and see how the other half lived. Unflattering as she found the term, she'd purposely gone slumming.

Now it seemed wrong.

She liked Carly. She liked Carly's life. She liked the people in Carly's life.

And she didn't know how to leave it.

Sean deepened the kiss, and with a helpless little moan, she gave in. Just this one last time, she thought greedily. Then she'd stop him, though it would be the hardest thing she'd ever done. She felt his hand on her hip, gripping her close. Heard his deep moan.

Dragging his open mouth along her jaw, he worked his way to her ear. "What is it about you?" he wondered roughly, his breath on her sensitive skin giving her a delicious shiver. "I can't keep my hands or my mouth off you." One hand stroked up her side. His mouth continued to explore her neck, her throat, nuzzling at the base of it, and Carly, melting, still shivering, tilted her head back to give him better access.

She wasn't a woman driven by lust. She'd kissed men before. She'd even slept with a few. All of it had been on her terms, at her convenience. She'd held the power and known it. She was decent looking, wealthy, and men liked that. They groveled for it.

Here, with Sean, she felt that power shift. *He* held it. *He* drove her. Here, she wasn't beautiful. She wasn't wealthy. She wasn't an instant icon. She was merely Carly Fortune.

And he still wanted her.

It was both freeing and terrifying. "Sean…"

His tongue stroked her skin, right where her neck and shoulder met, and her eyes crossed with lust. *"Sean."*

"Mmm. You taste good." He tasted her

again, and she heard her own moan. It was low and deep and throaty, and the pure need and hunger in the sound shocked her.

"This is not rational," he said. "It's definitely not smart. You're leaving, going back to your home, wherever that may be, and..." His fingers, his clever fingers stroked her belly, her ribs, dallied just below the curve of her breasts, which were already hard, already aching.

"Sean..."

"Where is that, Carly? Your home?"

"I—"

His mouth played with the corner of hers, nibbled and teased. His fingers danced across her ribs, even higher, and Carlyne nearly grabbed them and moved them up where she wanted them.

He looked at her, eyes hot, breath coming fast, his thumbs stroking the bottom curves of her breasts.

More, she almost cried. "I came here from my family's summer home in Spain."

His tongue caressed hers in a deep, long, rewarding kiss. And he finally, finally cupped her breasts. Pleasure flooded her.

"They must miss you."

She sank her fingers into his hair so he

couldn't pull back more because she wanted his mouth on her, not talking. "No."

"No?" Another kiss, a slow, long, wet, deep one that robbed her of thought. "I would miss you," he said.

"You're nothing like them." His thumbs were slowly gliding over her nipples, back and forth, making her gasp, making her writhe until her hips were undulating on the lounge.

"I'm not?" He stretched out over her, giving her his warmth, his weight. She could thrust against him, and he could thrust back. *Heaven*.

"Did they hurt you, Carly?" His hands slid beneath her sweater, his big, warm, work-roughened hands. "Is that why you don't like to talk about them?"

"What?" Was she supposed to be able to think with his hands on her?

"Your family. Did they hurt you?"

"No." She was nearing the cusp of oblivion, thrilling to his body on hers, his hands on her skin.

Then he tried to pull off her glasses.

"No!"

"It's just a pair of glasses."

"Yes." She wanted that oblivion! The promise in his body! "But—"

"You use them like a shield." He pushed up, bringing reality back with a cold dash, and looked at her with those dark, dark eyes. "You use the glasses and your clothes and your makeup. I feel like I don't even know what you look like, Carly."

"I'm just as I appear." God, it was almost true in a way. She'd nearly become Carly.

And if she took off the disguise, she wouldn't even know how to act.

She'd forgotten how to be Carlyne.

"Why don't I believe you?" he asked softly.

"I...don't know." Yes. Yes, she did know.

"I want you," he said with heart-wrenching sincerity. "I think you want me back. But this isn't going to happen without honesty."

Regret washed through her because she couldn't give him that honesty. She couldn't give it to him, and in return, he wouldn't give her what she wanted. *Him.*

When she remained silent, he stood. For a long moment, he looked at her, all the longing and yearning so evident in his gaze a mirror of her own.

Then he walked away.

NEARLY TWO WEEKS to the day after Stacy had changed Sean's life by leaving him Melissa, she called him long distance.

She'd called every few days to talk to her daughter, sounding both homesick and elated at the way her job was going, but never had she called in the middle of the night.

"You okay?" It was his first question. When she said yes, his second was, "When are you coming back?"

Today or tomorrow, he knew. Melissa would be picked up. Carly would go back to whatever life it was that she was so mysterious about.

His life would be back to normal.

He could work late again.

He could stop making sure there were vegetables and fruit at the house.

He could sleep whenever he wanted. Not do dishes. Leave the toilet seat up.

He couldn't wait.

But his sister hadn't said anything. "Stace?"

"Um, yeah. About that." She spoke in the little voice that always used to melt him, but he was unmeltable at the moment.

"Stacy. When are you coming back?"

"Well…the job has been extended."

"Extended as in a couple of hours, right?"

"Oh, Sean. I miss Melissa so much, I do, but they love my work here. My designs, the material, everything. And they want me to do an entire show. Me. They want *me*, Sean. I still can't believe it. I'm pinching myself to wake up, but I'm not dreaming."

Sean wished he was.

"Can you believe it?"

No, dammit.

"They really want me, Little Miss No One U.S.A.!"

And just like that, Sean's heart fell right to his toes.

"Sean?"

"It's great," he heard himself say. "Of course they want you. You're the best."

"No, I'm—"

"The best," he said firmly, willing her to believe it. Willing her the confidence she'd never had, the confidence he was supposed to have somehow given her but hadn't.

He'd tried.

But their parents had never really known what to do with their young, wild, carefree, trouble-bound daughter. Sean had been ten when she'd been born, already independent, so he hadn't spent that much time with her—until five years ago, when their parents had died one after the other.

Twenty-five years old. His own man. His own life. And yet he'd been left with this whimsical, fanciful fifteen-year-old on his doorstep. Sean hadn't known a thing about teenage girls, much less troubled ones, but they'd gotten to know each other pretty quick. Together they'd done the best they could, but deep down he knew a real guilt, for even his best had clearly not been good enough.

He hadn't managed to make Stacy believe in herself and her abilities.

"This is my future, Sean."

"I know."

"Do you think I could stay? Just for another week or so?"

"Another week?" His voice cracked on that one. "That's a long time, Stace. Melissa really misses you."

"I miss her, too, so much. She's doing okay?"

Sure. If he forgot about her destroying his office one-handed. If he forgot the fact that she had a cry that could crack glass and a temper that could headline any horror flick. But she also had huge, expressive eyes that looked at him as if he were the center of her universe. And a hug that got him every time. "She's doing good."

"I'm making money, and it's not flipping burgers. I can't get over that." She sighed with relief.

Sean stifled his own sigh. "We'll be here waiting."

SEAN WENT to work before dawn. He did some of his best thinking at work.

Fact was, he wasn't sure what to do. He wasn't sure about a lot of things.

Such as Carly.

But he was clear on one thing. They seemed to have a hormone problem around each other. It wasn't something he understood.

Until Tina, he'd had the occasional relationship, which included a date every week or so, the midweek phone call and some recreational sex.

Then Tina had come along, and he had fallen hard. After, he'd closed off his heart.

End of problem.

Ever since, he'd avoided complications. Simple enough. Whenever a woman wanted more from him, he felt claustrophobic. But this time there was no claustrophobia in sight, and this woman was *living* with him. What did that say?

The thought was nothing less than terrifying.

He could want her and not trust her, he told himself. He'd learned that much. Keep it simple. Easy. Light.

Yeah, no problem.

So why he canceled a meeting, didn't return phone calls, left Nikki with her mouth hanging open in shock and, for only the second time ever, went home early was beyond him.

So much for simple, easy and light.

He didn't want to think about why he was doing this. Except that when Melissa saw him walking up the porch steps, she squealed with such delight his heart squeezed.

Carly didn't squeal with delight, she didn't even smile, but something in the way she looked at him melted him anyway. He didn't want to be drawn to her, but it didn't seem to matter what he wanted. His brain was no longer in charge.

The unthinkable happened the next morning, Saturday.

He didn't want to go to the office. He wanted a weekend at home, no work, complete with relaxing. He wasn't sure what that entailed exactly, but he would figure it out.

It was early when he walked into the kitchen, but Melissa and Carly were already there. They stared at him in surprise.

"You're late for work," Melissa said, pointing her finger at him. "Bad boy."

"I'm not going to work."

Melissa grinned.

Carly went still.

"I'm taking the day off."

"To do what?" Melissa asked.

"Well..." He glanced at Carly, then laughed. "I'm not sure."

"I'll pack," Carly said quietly.

She thought it was over. And the two weeks were. His heart squeezed because he didn't want her to go. In spite of everything, he didn't want to say goodbye. "Yeah. About that—"

"Can we have a picnic?" Melissa demanded, oblivious to the tension around her.

"Just a minute, Melissa." Sean lowered his voice to a mere whisper for Carly. "My sister needs some more time."

"She's not coming back?"

He shook his head. "Not for at least another week."

She looked deep into his eyes for a long moment. "I didn't expect that."

"I know. Will you stay?"

Melissa was bouncing around at their feet. "So can we? Can we have a picnic?"

Carly was looking at Sean. "Yes," she said.

Melissa beamed, thinking she had her answer. "Yippee! A picnic!"

Carly avoided Melissa's gaze and started cleaning the breakfast dishes. "Have fun," she said.

Melissa threw her arms around Sean and gave him a sloppy, wet kiss on the cheek. "You're the bestest," she cried.

Sean wiped his slobbery cheek, smiled at Melissa, then moved behind Carly, who was washing a pan for all it was worth. "You game for a picnic?"

She looked at him, glasses fogged from the hot water, for once her mouth unpainted. She had a world of mistrust in her gaze. And a vulnerability that twisted at him.

"Come on," he coaxed. "I'm the bestest, you know."

She smiled at that. "Yes. Yes, you are."

Grinning, he bent to kiss her on the cheek. Just a little kiss. A little thank-you kiss.

Only Carly turned to look at him, and their mouths lined up.

Perfectly.

She made a little sound, and Sean pressed closer still, needing to hold that kiss for as long as he could. He might have stayed like that forever, except he became aware of a violent tugging on his pants.

"Kiss me, too!" Melissa yelled.

"Okay." Still stunned, Sean bent low, gave her a sweet little peck on the cheek.

"That's not the same!"

Carly let out a startled laugh.

And at the sound, Sean felt lighter than he had in a very long time. "No, it's not the same kind of kiss at all."

8

FOR THE FIRST TIME in Sean's life, he was attracted to a woman, and it had nothing to do with her physical appearance. He couldn't blow it off to...well, he didn't know exactly.

They saw a movie. Went on a picnic. Had a walk on the beach.

Melissa had a great day, and Sean had to admit, so did he.

It wasn't until he'd showered for the dreaded required cocktail party that night that work came into his brain. It almost seemed like an imposition.

He came out of the shower, reached for his clothes and stopped short. Would Carly have something to wear to go with him tonight? And how could he not have thought of it before?

He doubted she had much money, and she certainly didn't seem to have a wide variety of clothes.

Cursing himself, he slipped into his pants and went down the hall to her bedroom.

"Yes?" She didn't open the door to his knock.

"Can I talk to you?"

"Uh, now? I'm a little busy." She did sound rushed. "I'm trying to get ready."

"That's what I wanted to talk to you about. I might have forgotten to mention it's dressy...."

"You mentioned."

"Okay, well..." Ah, hell. "Carly, do you have something to wear?"

"Now's a fine time to ask," she said, but at least there was a smile in her voice.

"Yeah, I know. I'm sorry. So..." He stared at the closed door, feeling like an idiot. "Do you? Have something to wear?"

"Go away, Sean. I'll be ready in a second."

Yes, Carlyne had something to wear. But no, it wasn't going to be sleek and slinky and earth-stopping.

She looked at herself in the mirror and felt...plain.

It was new, this feeling, this not turning heads. Who would have thought she'd miss that? "Did you change your mind about taking me with you?" she called to Sean, not knowing if he still stood outside her door. In the mood for a little trouble, she hauled it open with a satisfying yank. "Because, if you did, that's really just fine with me—"

Oh, Lord.

He still stood there, wearing only his pants. His chest was wet, as if he'd showered and hadn't taken time to towel off.

Had he said his swimming was a stress reliever? Because man, oh, man, it had truly done wonders for his physique. Those broad shoulders, that sleek, smooth chest...

"I didn't change my mind about taking you," he said. A tiny rivulet of water ran down his jaw, dropped to his chest and slowly slid over his ribs, past that stomach she wanted to touch, and disappeared into his pants. They were open, proving he'd indeed been in some kind of hurry, and if there'd been better light in the hallway she might have gotten to see—

"Did you change yours?" he asked, his voice low and husky.

He'd seen her staring. And he was staring back. Only it wasn't in quite the same heated, hungry way, and she couldn't say she blamed him.

She wore a full black skirt, to the floor. The matching sweater was a zippered tunic, leaving her covered from chin to toe. It was purposely unrevealing and not even close to sexy. But it suited Carly.

If Carlyne had dressed like this, whoever her date was would have been bitterly disappointed, as she was known for her beautiful, sophisticated and naturally sexy style.

But Carly wasn't sophisticated.

Sean didn't look disappointed, though. In fact, he wasn't looking at her body at all, but into her eyes. She saw relief that she was going with him, and something else that made her breath catch.

Had she thought he *wasn't* looking at her with hunger and heat?

He was, oh, he definitely was, and it was her own little miracle.

"I just wanted to make sure about your dress," he said quietly. "I should have asked before now."

She'd done nothing to deserve it, and yet he cared about her. Another miracle. "Are you...going like that?"

Mischief filled his gaze. "Is that a problem for you?"

"Not for me. But you might find it tedious with all the women in the place following you around, drooling."

He laughed, looking a little embarrassed, which she found unbearably sweet.

The men in her world knew exactly how gorgeous they were.

"I'll be ready in five," he said.

In five minutes exactly, he met her in the foyer, and Carlyne nearly fell over.

She'd seen him in jeans. In casual wear. Oh, and his bathing suit, let's not forget that mouthwatering experience. But she'd never seen him dressed for success. Quite simply, he took her breath away.

"Okay?" he asked.

Okay? He could have walked right off the glossy pages of any magazine. "I, uh, yeah. You look…"

Mrs. Trykowski walked in the front door. "Beautiful!" She gave him an enthusiastic hug. "Only thirty years younger, Seany, my boy, and I'd go for you myself."

To Carlyne's amusement, he reddened as he kissed Melissa goodbye.

The little girl clung, throwing her arms around her uncle's neck. For exactly one second, Sean hesitated, as if surprised by her genuine show of love and affection. As if he didn't quite know what to do with all that emotion.

Over Melissa's head, he met Carly's gaze.

Just as baffled by matters of the heart, Carlyne lifted a shoulder and gave him a little smile. Closing his eyes, he wrapped his arms around Melissa and returned the hug.

It was a family moment, a special one. And suddenly she yearned for some of that same love and affection in her family.

But then Sean was taking her arm, leading her down the walk, and they were alone in his car.

He put the key in the ignition but didn't turn. Instead, he faced her, looked at her, *into* her. Unhappy in her get-up, especially next to his beautifully clad body, she wished he could see the real her, not this dowdy unsophisticated person she'd created. Wished he'd stop looking at her. *"What?"*

"You're beautiful."

With a snort, she pushed up her glasses and turned away.

His hand settled on her arm, and reluctantly she turned back.

"You are," he said quietly.

"We're going to be late."

"Carly..."

That name! "Please, Sean. Just drive. Let's get this over with."

For a moment, he looked at her, at her hair, her glasses, her mouth, then into her eyes. "We can talk later then."

"Maybe."

He started the car. "Definitely."

HALFWAY UP THE WALK to the sprawling beachfront house where the party was, Carlyne's deep skirt pocket started ringing.

It was her cell phone, which she was carrying because she still hadn't made her daily call to Francesca.

Sean stopped short and looked at her as if she'd grown wings. "Your skirt is ringing."

"It's nobody," she said, hoping Francesca—it had to be Francesca—would hang up.

"Why don't you take out the phone and say hello to nobody?" Sean asked.

"It's probably just a wrong number."

"Uh-huh." He reached into her pocket and took out the phone. Looking at the read-out, which had a caller ID, he frowned. "It's long distance. As in another country."

She grabbed the phone. "Hello, Francesca. Can you say *bad timing?*"

"Sorry, sweetie. I'm going to be out and didn't want to miss your call. How's your hunky boss?"

Carlyne pressed the phone closer to her ear and glared at Sean. "I never said he was a hunk."

He lifted a brow.

Francesca laughed. "You never had to.

You extended your stay. You wouldn't have done that for just anyone."

Was she so shallow that she wouldn't have helped a friend in need unless he fit a certain physical criteria? God, she hated facing that. "Well, I'm doing it now," she said stiffly. "And that's what counts."

"Yes," Francesca agreed sweetly. "And of course, with all this newfound righteousness, you've told him the truth."

"Um…" Carlyne looked at Sean.

He smiled.

Her heart went pitter-patter. She wanted him, no doubt. But she couldn't let herself have him under this pretense. It was wrong. "Tonight," she promised.

Francesca sighed with relief. "Call me if you need me."

"I will."

"Who was that?" Sean asked as she slipped the phone into her pocket.

It was time, past time, to come clean with the man she'd more than half fallen for. But in doing so, she very well might lose the best thing that had ever happened to her. "It was a friend of mine."

"Ah, you admit to having a life."

She had to smile. "Yes."

His eyes softened, and he cupped her face. "That's a start."

Because she had to, she went up on tiptoe and kissed him softly.

His thumbs stroked her jaw. "You keep doing that and we'll miss the party."

"That would be...lovely."

His eyes heated. "Say the word."

"Sean."

He slid his cheek to hers, nibbled at her ear. "You know where to find me when you're ready." He opened his mouth on her throat, and her eyes crossed with lust. "Are you?" He dragged that hot, wet mouth down her neck. "Ready?"

Judging by the weakness in every bone, *yes.* Judging by the throbbing between her thighs, double resounding *yes.*

"Your party," she mumbled. "You said it was required."

He lifted his head, looking frustrated and hot. Very hot. "After the party, then."

At the thought, the throbbing intensified. After the party they would do it all. Talk. Make love. Talk some more.

Or so she hoped, with all her heart.

THERE WAS MUSIC and laughter. Elegant, so-phisticated people milling around, talking about themselves. It should have been second nature to Carlyne, but it wasn't to Carly.

All she could think about was Sean. About tonight. Tense and edgy, she did her best to circulate when what she really wanted was some release to all this tension inside her. The music was classical, the food expensive and tasteful. The people were interesting.

And she couldn't breathe.

She escaped into the bathroom, turned on the light and stared at her reflection. What was the matter with her? She should have fit right in out there.

She'd been bred for such parties. Small talk, a distant smile…she had a talent.

But tonight she wasn't Princess Carlyne.

Tonight she was Carly, a woman who took care of a child for a living. A woman beginning to wish with all her might that this was really her life.

"Carly?"

At the light knock on the bathroom door and the unbearably familiar masculine voice, everything within her tightened in anticipation. Debating between what her brain knew to be best and what her body wanted, she opened the door a crack. Sean pushed in.

"Sean. What are you doing?"

He shut the door, then sent her a long, scorching look that told her exactly what he *wanted* to be doing. He was so big, so leanly muscled, so masculine. So gorgeous. And so utterly out of place in this ridiculously feminine bathroom.

Still holding her gaze, he engaged the lock.

"Um, Sean?"

"I can't breathe out there." He unbuttoned his jacket, slipped it off his shoulders and hung it on the hook on the back of the door. "You're supposed to be helping me, Carly."

"Yes. Well…" In his white dress shirt, he looked every bit as sophisticated and elegant as any aristocrat she'd ever seen. Then he smiled and took a step toward her. "I can breathe when I'm looking at you, Carly."

"Oh." It was the sweetest thing anyone had ever said to her. He pressed her against the counter, buried his face in her neck and rocked his body to hers. "Oh, my," she whispered.

She felt him smile against her neck as he slid his arms around her. "I've been wanting to do this all evening."

"We've only been here twenty minutes."

She gripped the counter behind her, which did two things. One, it gave her some desperately needed support, since her knees had refused to support her.

And two, it pressed her entire body against the length of his.

"I told you I hate these silly parties." His mouth found her ear. "You taste good."

"Sean—" She planted a hand on his chest and pushed, because she couldn't think with his mouth on her. "You're supposed to be out there socializing."

"I know." His hands were very busy, molding her hips, her spine, her bottom. "Oh, yeah," he murmured. "This is helping, believe me. Now tell me why you were hiding."

Capturing his hands, she let out a nervous laugh. "Somehow I lost my touch with this socializing thing. I'm no help to you here tonight. I'm sorry."

"It's easy, remember?" Sean's mouth followed the curve of her jaw. "Just carry a drink and smile."

He was mocking her. And kissing the corner of her mouth. His hands broke free from hers. One big, warm one skimmed up her cheek, and his fingers gripped the earpiece of her glasses.

He was going to take them off. Putting her hand over his, she waited until he lifted his head. "Sean..." The way he was looking at her was intoxicating, with all the dazed heat. "Not here."

"You feel it, too."

"I always have."

He went very still, then skimmed a slow hand up and down her spine. "I'm not sure what to do with all this wanting, Carly."

For the first time, the name Carly wasn't a heart stopper. It didn't make her sad, because suddenly she no longer yearned to hear him call her Carlyne. She liked Carly.

She wanted to be her.

Maybe, after she told him the truth tonight, she could find a way to make that happen, could find a way to meld both her lives together into one she could live with. In his embrace, she could almost imagine everything would be okay.

He bent his head and kissed her again, softly. "I can feel you," he whispered. "Your skin, your curves, your heat. Why are you hiding all that from me? Don't you know how beautiful you are?"

Tears stung her eyes. Had a man ever been so attracted to her? Never. And it was now, when she was looking about as bad as she could look, that it really hit home.

He wanted her no matter what she looked like. He was attracted to what she was on the inside. That simple. "Sean, we…need to talk."

"Hmm." He occupied himself with kissing her neck, then tugged away the sweater to expose more skin.

"Really. Talk first." But her voice was weak.

He found her collarbone, and she let out a helpless hum. He had one hand at the small of her back, urging her closer, his other slipping down, down, cupping her bottom while he slowly rocked his erection against her.

A hungry, desperate groan escaped each of them, interrupted by a knock at the door.

Slowly, very slowly, Sean lifted his head, his breathing rough and ragged. "Coming," he called, his voice a bit hoarse. "Let's go home," he whispered to Carly. "Now."

"To talk."

"To everything."

9

SEAN OPENED the bathroom door and stared into the startled faces of Sam and his wife, Helena. His hosts.

"Sean," Sam said with amusement.

Helena looked Carly over with interest and lifted a brow. She'd been trying to set Sean up with one girlfriend after another for the better part of a year. "Well, hello."

"Having fun, are we?" Sam asked with a wide grin.

"Sorry for the holdup. We…need to go."

"I see." Helena kissed his cheek. "Nice seeing you."

"Thanks." Sean took Carly's hand and led her through the crowded house toward the door.

They were stopped time after time by clients, friends of clients, would-be clients. Frustrated, he abruptly changed tactics and took them through the living room, which had been cleared to allow dancing. There, he headed toward the sliding glass door, which led to the open yard.

"Slow down," Carly whispered breathlessly.

On the patio, he turned, reached for her. Their bodies brushed together, then again, deliberately. He ran a hand down her back, urging her even closer. "I can't get you out of my head, Carly. How you taste, how you feel. The sounds you make when I touch you."

He was gratified to see her eyes glaze over. "Still want me to slow down?" he teased.

"No."

From the yard they could walk to the front, get in his car and get home. To his bed.

But the night was so lovely. Warm yet breezy, the air carried the scent of the ocean, which was just beyond the property past the bluffs. The sky was littered with stars, like diamonds on a blanket of black velvet. And the music, soft now, drifted over them. He pulled her into his arms.

"What are we doing?"

"Dancing." No hurry, he realized, because here, right here in the moment, was very nice, too. He took her hand, leading her off the lit deck into the shadows, where the grass was thick and luxurious beneath their feet, where the night shaded them from view. Her breath caught when he pulled her close, and at the sound, his entire body tightened.

"Sean—"

"Relax," he said softly in her ear.

"I'm going to have a little trouble with that," she said on a little laugh. "When I'm in your arms like this, I can't seem to think. Your body... Well," she said, sounding embarrassed.

"Don't stop there."

She gave a self-conscious smile that lit his heart. "My face feels hot, and the fire is spreading."

He hoped to put that fire out by the end of the evening. "Ease up against me." He let out a rough groan when she did. "Yeah. Like that." He'd never thought of her as a particularly petite woman. How could he when she'd always covered herself in so many layers? But here, now, with his hands roaming her body, she felt so slender, so feminine. His attraction to her hadn't had anything to do with her body, but now that it touched his like this, he changed his mind.

When he swayed, she swayed, and when he turned, she turned. Perfectly in sync, as if they'd been together forever. "You feel so good," he murmured, loving how her arms were tight around his neck, the way her breath brushed against his neck.

They stayed like that, closer than close, moving together sensuously, erotically, until finally the music stopped.

After a long, reluctant moment, she released him and stepped back.

"That was real nice, Carly."

"I don't know... Sean, I don't want this evening to be over. I don't want things to change."

There was a sadness in her eyes he didn't understand. "Why would they?"

"It's complicated."

No doubt. Everything good was. "One more dance," he whispered when the band started again, and when she hesitated he pulled her into his arms.

IT WAS RIGHT where Carlyne wanted to be, in Sean's arms. Oh, how she wanted that. It was a homecoming, a delicious cool drink after a day too long in the sun. His breath was warm against hers. His fingers slow and sure at the base of her spine, stroking softly, his strong legs pressed against hers.

And when he closed his eyes, pressing a sweet kiss to her temple, she nearly cried.

She'd never known such tenderness.

The wind teased their bodies. The night noises added to the beautiful, haunting music, to the scent of the sea, to the most amazing man in her arms. Her fingers played in his hair. Her other hand, entangled with his, lay against his thigh, which was taut.

Swaying softly.

Kissing lightly.

Touching gently.

Carlyne had danced with many, many men in her life. She'd been stepped on, hit on and had had to lead. But not with this man. Sean O'Mara was an extraordinarily sensual dancer, and for the first time ever, she became one, too.

It didn't take but a moment for the embrace to change, to deepen. Intensify. Until now, dancing had been only an obligation, something that was expected.

Now she wanted time to stand still.

Ragged breathing wasn't her only problem when they separated. She was on fire, burning and yearning. She, Princess Carlyne Fortier, wanted a man more than she wanted her next breath.

But she wasn't a princess, not in this moment. And in a way, she wasn't Carly, either. Didn't matter, she still had to tell him everything. And risk all. "Need fresh air," she whispered, and whirling, she walked off.

The grass was deep and thick, and not easy to maneuver through, so she bent and removed her shoes before speeding up her pace.

She had no idea where she was going.

When the grass turned to sand, she kept walking. When she topped the bluffs, she made her way down. And found herself on the beach.

The moon was hidden behind low, dark clouds, casting a beautiful blue glow on the waves pounding the shore.

And on the tall, beautiful man who'd followed her.

A small sound escaped her, one of loneliness, of wanting. She'd known he'd follow her. Maybe a small part of her had wanted him to.

Against her ribs, her heart beat a rapid tattoo. "I always wanted to live by the beach," she said.

"Ah. Something new about you." His lips formed a small smile as he moved closer. "Maybe one of these days you'll give me more than a hint here and there." He reached her, and very carefully, as if he expected her to run, took her hand firmly in his.

Tonight, she silently promised him as she went willingly against him. *Tonight I'll tell you everything.*

Including how much I love you.

She waited for him to speak, but he was silent. If she had to give him up, then at least she could have tonight. She would have tonight.

It would have to be enough.

As if Fate was on her side, the moon moved behind a long, low cloud, taking away the remaining glow, hiding them both in complete darkness.

In the black anonymity of night she could be Carly one last time.

When he reached out and took off her glasses, she let him. When he cupped her cheek, so lightly she might not have felt it at all if her senses hadn't been on red alert, she turned her head and kissed his palm.

At the change in his breathing, the knot in her belly increased. Then he tipped her face to his. She couldn't see his expression, but she could feel his heat, his need, and she met him more than halfway.

She would take this, take him, and treasure the memories for the rest of her life.

His mouth was as firm and sensual as his body, and he knew how to use both. His tongue slid along hers, his hands learning her body, and when he finally raised his head, she was panting for more.

"If I kiss you again, I won't want to stop," he warned.

There were a million reasons this was a bad idea, and yet she couldn't think of a single one. "Then kiss me again."

No second invitation required. The words were hardly out of her mouth before his mouth took hers in the hottest, wettest, most carnal kiss she'd ever engaged in. Then, before she could catch her breath, he'd scooped her up in his arms and carried her down the beach and around the edge of a bluff to their own private world.

Sean dropped his jacket to the sand, then sank down, pulling her with him. "You sure?"

Oh, yeah. She was sure. To prove it, she reached for the buttons on his shirt, spreading the material wide, dancing her fingers across his skin. There was something about not being able to see that heightened her sense of touch, her sense of smell. And he both felt and smelled like heaven.

With similar bluntness, he reached for the front zipper on her sweater. Slowly it parted, and he slipped his hands inside, guiding it off her shoulders and down her arms. Then her bra. "I wish I could see you," he whispered, laying her on her back on his jacket.

Before she could answer, before she could even think, *If you could see me, we wouldn't be doing this,* his mouth nuzzled at the sensitive spot between her neck and collarbone, then lower. Cupping her breasts, plumping them up, he bent his head and opened his mouth on one, sucking, teasing with his tongue and teeth. Lifting his head, he ran a thumb over the wet peak, back and forth.

She cried out. She couldn't help it. She was burning up from the inside out and needed him to put out the fire. Thrusting her hips helplessly against his, she continued making dark whimpering sounds she couldn't contain. "I've never felt like this," she said, horrified at the admission. "Never."

"I know."

Did that mean he'd never felt like this, either? In the months ahead without him, she would have liked to treasure the memory of knowing that. But he didn't say, just kissed her hard, fueling her desperation with his own.

Then he left her for a moment, surging up to take off his shirt, and for the first time she felt like cursing the dark because she wanted to see his naked body against hers. Impossible, of course, but she could *feel*, and she did just that, spreading her fingers wide to touch every part of him she could reach. His broad shoulders. His strong arms. His wide chest. And that stomach... It rippled and quivered when she surged up to place her mouth right next to his belly button.

His breath caught, and she found she loved that sound. When she reached for his pants with fumbling fingers, he helped her push them down. And then he was shoving up her skirt, reaching for her tights, then her panties, until finally, oh, finally, they were slick, heated skin to slick, heated skin.

There was no way to mistake his erection, no way she wanted to. Wrapping her arms around his neck, she breathed, "Now. Please, Sean, now."

She heard the sound of a foil packet opening and wanted to tell him to hurry, forget the condom, that for once, she wanted to be heart and soul with someone without any barriers between them, but she said nothing until he came back to her, pulled her close and entered her.

She cried out his name; he cried out hers. No longer could she think about her disguise or the dreaded condom or anything but how he made her feel, buried deep inside her.

He started to move within her, his rough, "Oh, yeah," echoing in her mind because it had never felt like this, never. Arching, lifting her knees to take him in deeper, deeper, *deeper*, she had the time to gasp his name before she burst out of herself.

It startled her, the ease of it, the pure pleasure, for she'd never come before without straining, without really working for it. Two more strokes and he came, too, her name on his lips. The feel of him, the sound of him, triggered yet another orgasm for her, and it went on and on until they collapsed against each other, damp and sated and stunned.

Sean stayed over her for a long, long moment, his arms quaking faintly. She savored the last bit of pleasure. When he finally pulled away, Carly rolled to her back and studied the dark sky. Sean came up on one elbow and looked at her, his dark gaze gleaming in the night.

"Okay?" he asked, his voice low and direct.

"More than okay." She already wanted to touch him again, desperately. Wanted him to touch her.

So when he slipped an arm beneath her, she eagerly turned to him, curving her body into his. She held her breath, knowing men didn't want to be clung to, but he didn't seem to mind at all. Her face was against his neck so that she could breathe in his scent. Her breasts were pressed against his chest. One of her thighs fell between his, as if their being tangled together, naked, on the beach, was the most natural thing in the world.

It felt so surreal, not being able to see him. Surreal to be stroking, exploring to her heart's delight, but she did it anyway. He seemed perfectly content to let her, as he had his own exploring to do. No part of her was left unstroked, unkissed.

She eagerly returned the favor. She found that when she slid a finger over his nipple, his breathing changed, shallowed. And that she could make him tremble by stroking a finger down his belly. When she cupped his sex, which was already hard again, he rolled her to her back, slid his fingers through hers and kissed her in an unrushed but heated way that brought the immediacy back between them.

"I have two more condoms."

Against him, she smiled. "Wouldn't want to waste them."

He nudged his erection between her thighs. "Now?"

"Oh, please, now."

Their joining was much more leisurely this time, but no less hot for taking their time. If anything, the feelings were intensified because of all the slow, heated touches and kisses and stroking. And this time, when they'd finished, they dozed off in the moonless night.

Carly woke some time later to Sean's hands on her body again. He seemed enthralled by her, which she understood, because she was equally fascinated with his body.

He ran his hands over her breasts, her belly, between her thighs. She came like that, then again when he moved inside her, thrusting with deep, rhythmic strokes.

Finally, sated and wobbling like drunks, they rose and faced each other, sharing a

kiss so sweet, so deep and tender, Carly felt
not only her heart but her soul stir.

And she both cursed and blessed the dark
that had saved her.

10

"MY GLASSES," Carly murmured, slipping them on quickly when Sean pulled them out of his pocket.

They could still hardly see each other in the thick blanket of night, but Sean was so attuned to her he found he didn't need to see her. Not that he wouldn't have loved taking her in the bright daylight, watching every nuance, every flicker of emotion that crossed her face as he kissed and licked and teased her to a screaming orgasm.

His body hardened at the thought.

Yep, definitely, he planned to do that.

But this had been incredible, too.

As he grabbed her hand, he felt her little shiver. She thrilled to his touch even now. It was a little unnerving, this connection.

Thunder cracked, startling them. Carly moved closer. Sean pulled her tight and kissed her. Which led to another kiss. And another.

Hearing the second, louder drum of thunder, she broke away from him with a nervous laugh. The single low cloud that had covered the moon had thickened during the time they'd spent on the beach. Time they'd spent lost in sexual pleasure.

Sean couldn't contain his very male, very satisfied grin.

"We'd better run for it," Carly said as a drop of rain hit her on the nose.

He licked it off, and while that turned to another hot, long, wet kiss, something was different in the heat and hunger streaking through his belly. It was deeper, more powerful. Heart-wrenching.

Which bothered him. This was not to have been deep or powerful. Definitely not to have been heart-wrenching. He didn't want her in his system. But he was beginning to understand that getting her out would be impossible. She was in his heart, and quite possibly there to stay.

He'd think of this later, *much* later. Right now he wanted to bask in the afterglow.

And maybe get some more. "Let's make a run for it."

By the time they climbed the bluff, the clouds were coming together with ferocious cracks of thunder, lit by razor-sharp strikes of lightning. The rain fell in earnest, big, fat drops.

Given the desolation and emptiness of the street in front of Sam's house, his party had broken up long ago. Drenched yet still exhilarated, Sean and Carly came to Sean's car. He searched his pockets.

"You found your condoms a lot faster than this," Carly teased as he fumbled for the key.

"I was in a much bigger hurry then." There was a streetlight illuminating them, and for the first time in hours he could see her face. Her makeup was smeared, her glasses askance. And her hair…it had long ago exploded out of its restraints and out of control. Her clothes looked heavy and cumbersome, especially now that they were getting wetter and wetter.

But her eyes were glowing, her smile was soft and special, and he knew she'd never looked more beautiful to him. "You look unbelievable," he whispered.

"Destroyed, more like," she murmured, brushing a hand over her hair, dropping her gaze from his.

"Ravaged," he agreed with a smile, letting her into the car. Bending, slipping his arms around her, he sucked a drop of rain off her bottom lip. "I like it."

She went still, staring deeply into his eyes, looking so solemn all of a sudden, so full of sorrow, his heart caught. "What's the matter?"

In a move that stirred his heart, she stroked his jaw and sent him a slow smile. "I'm just remembering this moment. I don't want to forget a thing. Not the way you touch me, the sound of my name on your lips, how you look at me, *nothing.*"

She spoke vehemently, as if what was between them was all over. "In my opinion," he said slowly, "this is just beginning."

She touched his mouth with her fingers, then kissed his jaw, still looking sad.

They got about a quarter of a mile down the isolated, narrow two-lane road before there was a loud pop.

Sean knew the sound and with a grim sigh pulled to the side of the road. "Flat," he said, and got out in the driving rain to fix it.

He'd removed everything he needed from the trunk and had bent to his task when he realized Carly was standing on the road alongside him.

"Here," she said, nudging the jack toward him.

Her hair was plastered to her face, and she had her arms wrapped around what he now knew to be a slender yet curvy frame.

"You're frozen," he protested. "Wait in the car."

But she squatted beside him. "Did you mean it?" she asked in a low, direct voice. "About this being just the beginning?"

Her eyes were huge behind the wet glasses, her body taut with...nerves?

"I meant it," he said with an ease that no longer startled him. "This isn't over just because my sister is coming back."

"Really?"

"Really. Now go stay warm in the car."

Instead, she went to her knees in the dirt beside him, reaching to stroke a strand of wet hair from his eyes. "You look very sexy all wet, Sean O'Mara."

"Yeah?"

"Oh, yeah." She wet her lower lip with her tongue.

He promptly dropped the jack and wondered if it was possible to do it in the back seat of a car filled with blueprints.

"If I help with the tire," she whispered in his ear, "we'll get done faster, which in my estimation—" she glanced at her watch "—would leave us with at least two hours of darkness left to do...well, whatever we pleased."

Sean broke the world record changing his tire with Carly's soft laughter egging him on.

"My, my." She handed him the wrench. "A man who can use his tools. I like that."

He was laughing when he kissed her. *Laughing.* He couldn't remember ever being turned on and full of amusement at the same time.

The thunder and lightning had stopped, but the rain hadn't. The side of the road where they'd parked had become a sea of mud.

If anyone had said he'd be changing a tire in the middle of the night, in the pouring rain, in a damn suit, and laughing while doing it, he would have called them crazy.

But here he was.

He wasn't thinking about work—not the getting of said work, or the doing of it, or the finding of it. In fact, around Carly, he almost always felt this way.

He liked that. Hell, he ran his own business, and he'd worked long, hard years for his success. If he wanted to cut back a little, if he wanted the weekends and evenings to himself, he was entitled.

And now he had someone to spend that time with.

They got back on the road, but hadn't gone far when they came to a small café with a Breakfast All the Time sign. Sean pulled in and turned to Carly.

She had a streak of dirt down one cheek, mingling with her running makeup, which made him grin. "I'm famished," he said. "How about you?"

"Pancakes sound like heaven," she admitted.

The rain hadn't let up, so they made a run for it, holding hands and laughing like a pair of kids.

Sitting at a booth toward the back, Sean pushed away the newspaper that had been left on the table, the one that had Princess Carlyne Fortier's face plastered across the front page.

They both blinked like owls in the garish, obnoxiously bright café, which was decorated in equally eye-squinting red vinyl and checked floors. But the scents coming from the kitchen had Sean's mouth watering.

Until he caught a good close look at Carly for the first time since they'd left Sam's party.

"I'm going to have bacon, too," she said,

scanning the menu, oblivious to his sudden stillness. "Tons of it. Crispy," she added with a grin that slowly faded when she realized he was staring at her. "What?"

His heart had stopped, but now it started up again with a funny rhythm that hurt with each beat, so he was mildly surprised to find he sounded so normal. "Where are your glasses?"

Her hand went immediately to her face, which turned ashen beneath the dirt and makeup. "I don't know."

He stared at her because it wasn't just the glasses, it was...

"I...must have lost them when we were changing the tire," she said, her words picking up speed as she went. She scooted to the edge of the booth and started to get up, but he put a hand on her wrist to stop her.

"Your eyes." He had to pause to take a deep breath. Something awful was happening as he stared at her, something so beyond his comprehension that his brain refused to put it together for him. "One is blue, like always. The other is...green. Carly, your eyes are different colors."

She closed her eyes, and when she answered, her mouth trembled. "I didn't realize I'd lost a contact, as well."

"They're really...green?"

Her eyes opened, but at the look on his face, she covered her mouth with a shaking hand and nodded. Belatedly, her other hand went to the top of her head.

"Too late," he whispered hoarsely. "I can see the blond poking out from under the wig I didn't know you wore."

A funny sound escaped her, one that told him exactly how miserable she was, but since he felt worse, *had* to feel worse, he didn't sympathize. "Why are you wearing a wig? And why do you need both glasses *and* contacts?" But he knew, God help him, he knew. He grabbed the newspaper, holding it up to compare the two faces, one so poised and elegant, one so grim and miserable. "You've purposely disguised yourself."

"Sean—"

"Coffee, folks?" Their waitress appeared and smiled at them, oblivious to the tension humming between them. "Or would you like to order?"

Order? He wanted to throw up. He tossed the paper aside. "We need a minute," he managed to respond.

"Of course." The woman started to walk away but glanced at Carly.

Her double take might have been comical

if this nightmare hadn't been happening to Sean.

"Why, I don't believe it! It's you! You've been hiding out here on the west coast? Oh, I *knew* it!" She let out a happy little squeal. "I told Marge just this morning you weren't any junkie in rehab. So...are you enjoying your stay?"

The clues had been there all along, of course. Her desperation for a job that supposedly had nothing to do with needing money. The way she always looked when she saw her reflection in a mirror—so utterly surprised.

And then of course, the whopper—her secrecy about her past.

"I'm an idiot," he muttered.

The woman he'd just made wild love to, the one clenching the menu, with her wig falling off and her eyes mismatched, winced. "Could we have a moment, please?" she asked the waitress.

"Of course!" Grinning, she bent close to Sean. "I won't tell a soul about your little romantic tryst," she promised in a stage whisper. "Honest."

When she was gone, he looked right into one green and one blue eye and said, "You're looking like quite a different woman than I started out with tonight. *Princess*."

She closed her eyes, both of them, and looked so miserable, so hurt and vulnerable that he hurt, too. But he didn't want to hurt. He'd promised himself he wouldn't ever hurt again. So he found his anger and let it override any sympathy he might have had. "Don't tell me. You're suffering amnesia. You've forgotten your real name."

Her eyes flew open. "I never forgot anything."

"Except to mention it to me."

"Oh, Sean." In spite of the multicolors, her eyes softened. "I wanted to tell you."

"Please."

"I did! I was going to tell you tonight, after the party."

"Before or after I made you come half a dozen times in the sand?"

She looked at the table, a flush working its way up her face. "I didn't know we were going to do that."

He jabbed a finger toward the paper. "How I didn't see it is beyond me. So what were you doing here? Was I your latest charity case? Screw a lonely architect? Make his week? What?"

"No!" She shook her head. "God, Sean, it wasn't like that."

From the counter, there came a clatter of a tray being dropped. The three waitresses in the café, one of them theirs, were all on the other side of the Formica counter, unabashedly eavesdropping.

So much for secrecy.

Sean stood and tossed a few bills on the table.

"Sean? Where are you going?"

If he hadn't known she was a liar, he might have believed the note of total panic in her voice. "Home," he said wearily.

"You're just going to leave me here?"

Princess Carlyne, or what he knew of her anyway, was a strong, independent, very capable woman. Carly Fortune wasn't so different. Look at what she'd managed to do to his life in only a few weeks. "I think you can manage," he said.

"I want to go home with you."

"No."

"You have my things."

Well, hell. "Fine." Purposefully distancing himself, he stood back to let her go first. He didn't touch the small of her back as they walked out of the café he'd never forget. He didn't so much as smile when she looked at him over her shoulder. He did hold open the car door, but he did it politely, and he didn't kiss her as she got into the car, though she was close enough, and just an hour ago he would have.

She tried to stop him, put a hand on his arm. He quivered at her touch and shrugged her off.

"Sean—"

"I don't want to hear it, Carly. Or should I say Princess?" Disgusted with both of them, he shoved the door closed.

They drove home in utter silence. His life would never be the same, and the pathetic thing was, he had no one to blame but himself.

11

MRS. TRYKOWSKI greeted them with a smile that faded as soon as she saw Sean's face. "What's wrong?"

"Thank you for tonight," he said, ignoring her question. He pulled some money out of his pocket, but the older woman shook her head, refusing to take it.

"I don't want money for watching your darling niece." Slowly, she divided a glance between Sean and Carlyne, who wanted to die of mortification because she knew exactly how she looked.

Like a circus performer.

"Oh, dear," Mrs. Trykowski said with a sigh. "The jig is up, huh, dear?"

Carlyne gaped at her. "You knew?"

"I have eyes in my head, don't I?" Turning to Sean, she lifted a finger and wagged it in his face. "And if you search your heart, you'll realize it doesn't matter, Seany, my boy. She's still a ten, and she's still the one for you. So don't you go doing something stupid now."

"Wait. *She's* the one who lied, and you're getting mad at *me*?"

"You're the male, aren't you?" With a secret smile aimed at Carlyne, she left.

Leaving Carlyne alone with Sean. She was so cold. Cold and sad. Oh, and destroyed, let's not forget that, because in one foolish move she'd blown her chance for anything and everything she'd ever wanted.

She started to shake, though whether it was the chill, her wet clothes or grief, she hadn't a clue.

Sean took one look at her, one really long look from head to toe. It was a look that might have made her melt with longing only a couple of hours ago, except all that heat she'd come to know had turned to quiet fury.

"Go change," he said roughly, then turned away.

Her clothes weighed a ton, but she hadn't explained, they hadn't talked. Without knowing how to make this right, she followed him.

He went into Melissa's bedroom. Kneeling by the bed, he reached out and smoothed the little girl's covers, then gently touched her cheek.

Carlyne couldn't see his expression, but there was tenderness pouring from him. Tenderness and tension.

Tension she'd given him.

Standing, he brushed past her and moved out of the room.

She caught up with him in the hallway. "Sean."

Shocking her, he stopped, and she wondered how to begin. "We need to talk about it."

Jaw tight, face grim, he sighed. "You're shaking, dammit."

"Because I'm afraid."

A frown curved his mouth downward. "Not of me. I would never hurt you."

"I'm afraid I'm going to lose the best thing that's ever happened to me."

"Don't." His eyes closed, and she briefly glimpsed a world of pain behind his controlled temper. "I don't want to talk about it."

But she needed to. Needed to tell him how she'd meant to come clean sooner but hadn't known how, needed to tell him how much she cared about him. "I—" A terrible bone-shaking tremor struck her, and she had to clamp her mouth shut, wrapping her arms around herself.

Sean turned away. "Go to bed, Carly. *Princess*," he corrected immediately. "You can wait until morning to leave."

But she couldn't move.

"Go on," he said harshly, and when she looked at him, he swore the hallway blue. He stalked toward her and swung her into his arms. Without a word, he strode into his bedroom, his arms taut and quivering with tension.

Or maybe it was her quivering.

Both miserable and in heaven, she laid her head on his shoulder. "I'm so sorry," she whispered. "I never meant to hurt you. I just wanted—"

"Save it." He practically dropped her to the bathroom floor in his rush to get his hands off her. "You're frozen solid." He flicked on the hot water. "Get in the shower and warm the hell up."

She stared at the steaming shower, everything blurring because of the tears she refused to shed. She'd brought this on herself. There was no one else to blame.

Somehow she'd broken all her rules. She'd fallen in love with Melissa. She'd fallen in love with Sean, a man who represented every part of every fairy tale she'd ever told herself. He was strong and independent with a sense of humor and a mind of his own. A man who might have even loved her back—as Carly.

How ironic was that? She'd finally found herself locked in Carly's persona, and now that woman was gone, as well. Now she was a woman halfway between. A woman who would be happy to spend the rest of her life this way, with a small, intimate family who loved her. *Her.*

"Get in the shower, Princess."

"Carly," she whispered.

"*Carlyne.*"

"I want to be Carly." She tried to unzip her sweater, but her fingers were shaking so badly it took her a moment to get a good grip.

"Dammit." Apparently unwilling to wait, Sean shoved her hands away and tugged the zipper down, parting the sweater, exposing her pale skin to his gaze for the first time. Ever. One more tug, and the water-soaked weight fell off her arms. As he already knew, her silky white bra had a front clasp. It was also wet, which left the material so sheer she might have been wearing nothing.

Jaw clenched, Sean opened that, too, and with a deep, ragged breath, peeled it away from her skin.

Her nipples were two hard, aching peaks. He closed his eyes but didn't say anything. She thought she heard a soft moan escape his lips, but she couldn't be sure. "Sean—"

"*Don't.*"

Her skirt came off next and, kneeling on the floor, he went after her boots, leaving her in thick tights and panties.

The tights had to be peeled away one leg at a time. The feel of his fingers on her, the way his dark head bent to his task, the way he held his breath, all combined to string her so tight she thought she might snap. Her heart certainly hadn't gotten the message that he would never again touch her the way he had on the beach, because it was racing in anticipation. Her every nerve had done the same, so that a simple stroke of his hand down her leg caused her to tremble all the more.

Finally, he slid his hands up her thighs and hooked his thumbs in the sides of her panties.

She stared at him, not breathing.

He stared at her, his breathing rough and uneven.

As the air danced over her wet, chilled body, she really did get cold.

But his hot gaze warmed everywhere it landed, and it landed plenty. No matter what he *wanted* to feel, he still desired her. He couldn't hide that.

He wasn't immune! It gave her a surge of hope, because he couldn't both hate her and want her, too, could he? No, she decided, he couldn't. Maybe it would have to start from physical release, his forgiving her. She'd appeal to him on an emotional level after, when he was ready.

Slowly he skimmed the panties down her legs, and if she'd expected him to avert his gaze, he didn't. He looked right at her, all over her, and along with her trembling came a need she'd never known before.

He couldn't have missed how aroused she was, not from his vantage point with her breasts just above his head, nipples thrust out, hard as stones. Between her legs she felt her own creamy wetness, which had absolutely nothing to do with the rain.

Standing there, completely exposed to his hot, hungry, angry gaze, she felt yet another powerful shudder go through her.

Suddenly, he surged up, pulled off her black wig and dropped it to the floor. She didn't know what she expected, but it wasn't for him to slip his fingers into her real hair. He massaged her head for a moment. She let out a soft sigh. Then, with hard eyes and grim mouth, he stepped back and opened the shower door.

He was going to shove her into the shower and pretend none of this existed between them. He was going to shut the door on her and walk away. She couldn't let him, so she wrapped her arms around his neck and pressed close.

Swearing again, he slipped his hands around her waist, lifted her and turned toward the open shower door.

And for that one second, when she was plastered against him, she closed her eyes and savored the feeling. Her thighs, her belly, her breasts were all smashed against his wet, cold clothes, but the sensation of being so open and vulnerable, of being completely naked to his fully clothed body, was startlingly arousing.

His eyes were tightly closed, as if he was trying not to feel her.

So she wriggled. A lot. Wrenching another curse from him.

"Be still, dammit." But he couldn't deposit her in the stall without getting into the shower himself, so they hovered there.

"Sean—"

"Quiet."

"There's only one way to make me quiet," she whispered, and brazenly slid herself over the bulge straining the fly of his pants.

A strangled sound escaped him. "I am absolutely not having sex with you."

Sex. That's what it had been to him.

To her, it had been much, much more. And she might have had a chance at making him think so, too, except for her deceit.

Swallowing hard, she leaned forward, pressed her bare breasts to his chest and was gratified to see his jaw clench. "I hurt you, Sean. I'm sorry. Please, let me tell you about it."

"I knew something was off," he said with a shake of his head. "I just kept excusing it, excusing you." A mirthless laugh escaped him as he looked into the spray of water. "Joke's on me. Again."

"I reminded you of Tina. Mrs. Trykowski told me what she did to you," Carlyne said when his head whipped toward her in angry surprise. "She told me you locked your heart up after that, and—"

"Not good enough, I didn't." He gave a cynical smirk.

She'd have to show him how good it could be, if he'd just give them a chance. Gently, she nibbled at a corner of his mouth. Then the other corner.

"No," he said, much less convincingly, and she tilted her head to the side to deepen the kiss, using her lips, her tongue, her heart and soul to tell him what he had to know—that no matter what she'd done, she still loved him, she'd always love him. He moaned and gripped her body tight as if he meant to pull away.

She softened their connection, tender and gentle, because she knew that was the true way to his heart, not aggression or heated passion, which he could have gotten from anyone.

He moaned again, then again when she used her hands, dancing them over his shoulders, his arms, anything she could reach, until finally he stepped with her into the shower fully dressed.

Wrapping her arms tighter around his neck, she breathed his name, but his eyes were tightly closed, his face a mask of agony and indecision.

He was still going to change his mind.

So she kissed him again, kissed him and slid down his body so she could start on the buttons of his shirt. He resisted, standing still and rigid as she kissed every inch of skin she revealed when she tugged his shirt down his shoulders, letting it fall to the shower floor, until he let out a helpless sound of pleasure and lent his fingers to the cause. His pants came next, and she went to her knees to drag them down his legs. Again, she kissed what she exposed, starting with a lean hip, a tense thigh, the spot between the two...

She'd barely gotten started when he lifted her, pressed her back against the wall and slid a hand between her thighs. Already he knew her, knew exactly where to touch to make her insides burn and her bones dissolve.

He opened his eyes, lifted his head and watched her with dark intensity as he slowly and purposely brought her to the very edge.

Her eyes fluttered closed.

"No," he said in a rough whisper. "Don't you hide from me, not ever again. Open your *green* eyes and look at me, dammit. Show me you, the real you this time."

"It is me," she gasped, because his touch

was her world at the moment. "It's always been me."

"But I've never seen you. Not like this."

His fingers never changed their rhythm. On the very verge of coming, she could hardly hear or see past the roaring in her head, past the raging need. "I...I can't stand, Sean."

Still stroking her, he wrapped his other arm around her waist and lifted her up, bracing her between the wall and his body, completely supporting her weight. "Do you want me?"

"Yes!"

She barely had time to spread her thighs wide when he thrust inside her with a single powerful stroke.

Instant orgasm.

When she could breathe, she blinked him into focus, his wet body, dark hair and those direct, intense eyes.

Still buried deep inside her, filling her to near bursting with his hot, throbbing length, he demanded, "What the hell do I call you?"

Spread wide, open to the touch of his body and his gaze, she couldn't recover. Little aftershocks were still rocking her body. "What?"

"Your name," he said roughly. "What do I call you?"

Oh. *Oh.*

Carly.

Carlyne.

Her deception, his pain.

Her own pain.

If she stopped to think about what would happen after tonight, she'd lose it, but she still had this, she had right now. And right now he was deep inside her, pulsing, hard as steel, with his hands all over her.

"Carly," she whispered, choking back a sob. "I want to be Carly."

"Carly," he said thickly, withdrawing from her slowly only to plunge back inside.

He kept touching her, everywhere, and her insides started a deep trembling she couldn't control. Unbelievably, she was going to come again. Her eyelids fluttered, but she forced them open so she could meet his gaze and see everything he felt, let him see everything she felt.

Another slow, purposeful stroke, and she was lost. She was always lost with him.

And when she was with him, she was found.

12

SHE WENT TO BED alone and woke up alone.

Princess Carlyne Fortier had definitely outstayed her welcome. Maybe Carly Fortune never would have, but that was a moot point now, wasn't it?

Sean had learned the truth, and he'd clearly decided that not only couldn't she be trusted, but she was far more trouble than she was worth.

It shouldn't have been a surprise. After all, no one in her life had ever wanted her just for her. Why should now be any different?

Getting out of bed and back into the shower reminded her of Sean. In fact, she thought, gliding the soap over her body, she might never have another shower without remembering how he'd taken her the night before, how he'd touched and kissed her as if his life depended on it.

Hers certainly had.

But afterward, he'd still refused to talk.

He'd sent her to bed and hadn't come back to her.

Carly hadn't expected to sleep, but she had. And now the house was awfully quiet. Too quiet.

She threw on clothes, raced down the hallway and came to a skidding halt in the kitchen. At the back door, with a big bag on one shoulder and Melissa in his other arm, stood Sean.

"You changed your hair!" Melissa cried, pointing. "It's yellow and all cut off!"

Sean said nothing, his eyes cool and distant.

Carly fingered her short blond bob. She'd never colored her hair and always went for the low-maintenance type of cut, because fussing with it was a low priority. Not to mention she hated wasting time at the salon.

Most would be shocked at that fact, expecting her to enjoy the pampering.

"Pretty," Melissa said. "You coming?"

"Where are you going?"

"Work," Sean said curtly.

One more minute upstairs and she would have missed them.

"I get to go today." Melissa beamed. "If I don't touch anything."

"I thought you'd be going back," Sean said. "So I'll take her with me."

Her heart had dropped to her toes. "Back?"

"To your life," he said. "After all, the game is over, isn't it?"

She struggled with her composure and failed. "It was never a game. You'd know that if you would let me talk to you."

"Yeah, well, I've got to go." He opened the door, but at the last minute turned back.

Her heart returned to its proper place because he was going to change his mind. They were going to talk.

"Bye, Carlyne," he said quietly.

"*Carly,*" she whispered, but he was gone.

As always, she was left alone, all because of who she was.

When would she learn?

Lifting her chin, she went to her room for her purse. She didn't want Carly's things. They could stay. She'd come to prove she could make it in the real world, but instead she'd learned an important life lesson.

She was on her own.

And she'd survive.

NIKKI STARED at Melissa as Sean walked into his office. "Where's the sexpot nanny?"

"Watch your language," Sean said, and set down the wriggling Melissa. "And she wasn't a sexpot."

"Uh-huh."

Sean looked at Nikki in exasperation. "She wore huge, baggy, shapeless clothing, long hair that hid her face and too much makeup. How is that a sexpot?"

"Because you couldn't keep your eyes off her."

Hard to argue the truth, so he turned away from his too-knowing assistant and looked for Melissa, who for a little thing had disappeared awfully quickly.

"Quick," Nikki warned, pointing at the blond head bobbing its way across the room. "Never mind, I've got her."

Melissa was zeroing in on the candy jar on Nikki's desk.

Nikki beat her to it. With a triumphant smile, she set the jar in her desk drawer and turned the lock. "Not anywhere near my desk, you don't."

Melissa folded her arms and stuck out her lower lip.

"Try it on someone who falls for the act, kid. So…" Nikki looked at Sean. "Where is she? Parking the car, right? She'll be here any second to take over—"

When Sean shook his head, Nikki groaned. "What happened?"

"Nothing. Everything," he added miserably.

"See?" she cried. "*This* is why messing around with co-workers is such a bad idea."

"Tell me about it."

Nikki put her hands on her hips. "Just answer me one question. Why? Why did you have to blow it with her before your sister got back? You only had, like, what? A few days left?"

"How do you know *I* blew it?"

"Because you're the guy, slick. Guys are always the one to blow it." She sighed loudly and looked at the still-pouting Melissa. "Okay, missy, listen up. No candy. No feeding the CD player. No touching any buttons on anything, especially the telephone. Keep that in mind, and we'll all get along. Got it?"

Melissa thought about that. "How about all those pretty colored pens in your desk?"

"The Hi-Liters? Consider them yours, if you color only on the paper I give you. Deal?"

Melissa smiled her killer four-year-old bargaining smile. "Ice cream?"

"You haven't had lunch yet."

"We could have ice cream for lunch."

"Nope."

"For dessert?"

"If the ice cream truck comes by."

Melissa's smile spread. "'Kay."

With some relief, Sean went into his office, determined to keep himself so busy he couldn't think.

It turned out to be impossible. Oh, he could keep busy, no problem. Melissa was helpful in that area, running both Nikki and himself ragged with terrifying ease.

But the thinking part...he couldn't seem to stop himself.

And busybody Nikki was no help.

After awhile, she popped her head into his office. "I've got Melissa counting paper clips." Getting comfortable, she leaned against his desk. "So...what did you do to Carly?"

Other than take her three times on the dark beach, then yet again in his steamy shower, all in ways that were going to fill his dreams with heat and longing for years to come? "Nothing."

"Melissa said you fired her because she changed her hair color."

"I didn't fire her."

"But she changed her hair color?"

"Nikki."

Ignoring his warning tone, she sank into a chair and looked at him expectantly.

He sighed. "She's Princess Carlyne Fortier."

Nikki's eyes widened. "Wow, this is better than my soap opera. I thought she was at a retreat or something."

"Or something." He scrubbed a hand down his face. "For whatever reason, she was hiding out here. With me. Playing at being a nanny."

Nikki frowned. "I don't think she was playing, Sean. She seemed really into Melissa. And you," she added. "I don't think she could have faked that. So why did she do it?"

"I don't know."

"What did she say when you asked her?" At his silence, she groaned. "You didn't ask her."

"No."

"Sean!"

"Well, why the hell would she have wanted to be a nanny, anyway?" She was hot. Beautiful. Sexy. Intelligent. It made no sense at all.

And why did he even care? She'd lied. Used him.

Hurt him.

"Maybe she wanted a break from her life," Nikki suggested.

"Yeah, all that money must be tiresome." He thought of what he'd paid her and was embarrassed. It had been a very fair salary, but he hadn't known she was a damn princess. To her, it would have been pocket change. "Look, she *lied*, Nikki."

"Ah."

There was a volume of knowledge in that *ah*. "What does that mean?"

"Sean," she said gently. "Not all women lie just to screw with you. Carly is different than Tina. Tina hurt you just because she could. That was the kind of woman she was. I think Carly, on the other hand, probably has a good reason."

Maybe. But regardless, he'd really fallen for her. And when they'd made love, he'd felt the earth move.

Hell, he was so confused. And more hurt than he could have believed possible, especially when he'd promised himself never to get hurt again. "Whatever her reason, she's gone."

"She just…left?"

"Well…"

"Sean!"

"Okay, so maybe I told her she'd be wanting to go back now."

"You kicked her out? You poor, stupid idiot. Did she even hesitate?"

No, he wanted to say, but that would be a lie of his own making. Truth was, she *had* hesitated. The look she'd given him when he told her to go home had twisted his heart before he'd managed to harden himself. "She might have hesitated. A little."

She shook her head. "And now you'll never know what could have been."

Now he'd never know. He'd never know if what they'd shared had been real or fake. He'd never know if she might have wanted to stay. He'd never know how she might have reacted if he'd told *his* truth, that he'd fallen in love with her.

He'd never know any of it.

FRANCESCA picked Carlyne up at the airport. She didn't ask for conversation, which was good, as Carlyne didn't have anything to say.

"Your family is thrilled you're going to be able to make it to the party tomorrow night," Francesca told her.

Her grandfather's eightieth birthday. It was going to be a huge event, with celebrities and politicians from all over the world. She'd be expected to greet guests, start conversations and keep everything running smoothly. She'd certainly be expected to smile a lot.

How could she do that?

Francesca looked over, saw her eyes fill and squeezed her hand. "I'm sorry."

"Thank you." God, she missed Melissa. She missed Santa Barbara. She missed the ocean. She missed the freedom.

She even missed Mrs. Trykowski.

But most of all, she missed Sean. He had made her smile, had made her laugh. He'd made her *live*. "I'm just tired," she whispered, her voice wobbly. "Very tired."

Leaning back, she closed her eyes. But all she saw was Sean, and the way he'd held her, as if she was the most important person in the entire world.

And for her short time with him, she had been.

TWO DAYS LATER Stacy came back for Melissa.

Sean had expected to feel great elation. *Freedom*.

Instead, his house was too quiet. He no longer had a bossy little girl demanding kisses. He no longer had a hot woman demanding kisses.

He was lonely, dammit. And he had no idea what to do about it.

13

"YOO-HOO!"

Sean got out of his car and waited for Mrs. Trykowski to leap over her flower bed and waddle up to him. He waited because it wasn't worth the effort to outrun her.

Not that he could have, because the woman, old as she was, moved faster than anyone he knew.

"Hello, dear," she said. "I saw Carlyne on the news. She's home, back in France with her family. Why is that, exactly?"

Yeah, Sean, why is that? "Because that's her home, Mrs. Trykowski. This was temporary, remember? A nanny job, and Melissa is gone."

"Pah."

"Excuse me?"

"She was more than a baby-sitter, Sean O'Mara, and you know it. How badly did you screw it all up?"

He stared at her. "Are you by any chance related to my assistant, Nikki?"

"I do not know any Nikki, but I do know that you are an idiot if you let her go home without telling her how much you love her."

"Look, I have to go to work," he said, rubbing his aching temples.

"Sure. Bury yourself in work again."

"I'm not the one who lied."

"Oh, get over it." Mrs. Trykowski waved her arms when she spoke, nearly hitting him in the nose. "If you lived the life she did, you'd want your peace and quiet and privacy, too! You ever think of that?"

No. No, actually, despite devouring every bit of news on Princess Carlyne he could since she'd left, he hadn't.

"If you'd needed to get away that badly, you would have done whatever you had to, which might just include putting on a wig and glasses and going to the other side of the world." Her eyes narrowed. "Face it, Sean. She acted human."

When she walked away from him, Sean stared after her, wondering how he'd become the bad guy. And why everything she'd said made far too much sense.

CARLYNE SAT in her Paris office and stared out the window. But instead of the buildings and streets crammed with people, all she saw was the Pacific Ocean, the beautiful sand and bluffs.

And Sean. She saw Sean.

"Daydreaming again." Francesca walked in and tsked but sent her a sympathetic smile. "Overwhelmed?"

It felt strange to speak in her native tongue, French, after so many weeks of English. "I can't find the invitation for the Driskel fund-raiser."

"It's on your desk."

"Oh. Well, I can't find—"

"It's on your desk."

Carlyne glanced around her at all the piles she thought she'd gone through. "And the—"

"On your desk." Patiently, Francesca sat. "Everything you need is on your desk."

Baffled, Carlyne lifted her hands. "So why does it all seem out of place?"

"Because *you're* out of place."

Carlyne stared at her, then sat back and let out a long sigh. "I know. It just all seems…" She waved a hand at her huge office, at the decadent interior she'd inherited from her mother when she'd taken over the job as Official Fortier Party Maker. "Big. *Too* big. It's a waste. I don't need this office."

"Probably not."

Carlyne shook her head. God, how she wanted the simple life back, the one she'd had with Melissa and Sean.

Francesca leaned forward and patted her hand. "You know, it's been nearly two weeks. You could just do as normal women do these days and call him."

"Who?"

Francesca gave her a dry look. "Gee, I wonder."

But he'd asked her to leave. How could she call?

"You never explained," Francesca said gently. "Calling to try to do so would be normal, Carlyne. Really."

"I've never been normal."

"Well, that's true. But in this case, you should make an exception. It's clear you're not going to be able to go on until you do."

"I should have told him the truth in the beginning."

"Yes," Francesca agreed. "But you didn't. So you'll have to make him understand now."

How? How could she make someone like Sean, a man who followed his own rules and never let others live his life for him, understand?

"Look, it's lunchtime," Francesca said. "I'm going to eat. Can I get you something?"

At the thought of food, her stomach rolled, which shocked her, because she loved to eat, always.

"Carlyne? You're looking green. You okay?"

No. No, she wasn't okay. She was nauseous and overly emotional.

Understandable, she assured herself. Sure, her period was late, but that was stress.

Sean hadn't used a condom in the shower.

Carlyne took a long look at her stomach. Flat.

Good.

Suddenly she could see herself big and round with pregnancy. Could see herself giving birth. Holding her baby. Loving that baby with all her heart and soul. Always being there for him or her. Always.

"Carlyne?"

"Nothing for me, thanks." She managed a smile. "Don't worry, I'm fine."

"If you're sure…"

"Very." She wasn't pregnant, couldn't be. Still, she couldn't contain that very small burst of hope. After all, she loved Sean. She'd love his baby.

Actually, at the moment she loved everyone and everything. She virtually danced over to Francesca to hug her tight.

"What was that for?" Francesca asked, squeezing her.

"Just because."

Carlyne waited until her assistant left before grabbing her purse and keys. She needed a drugstore.

And a pregnancy kit.

AFTER WATCHING the news and seeing Princess Carlyne Fortier's face everywhere, Sean had to admit Mrs. Trykowski had been right.

Carly—and he liked to think of her as Carly—was rarely smiling, and when she did, the smile didn't come close to her eyes.

She looked tired, haggard. Miserable.

It drove him crazy that no one, not her family, not the news anchors, not the reporters...*no one* commented on it.

How could he be the only one in the whole damn world worried about her?

She hadn't set out to hurt him. He really believed that. He believed her lies had had nothing to do with him.

And if he believed that, then he had to believe she hadn't been merely slumming, playing around with his feelings.

But what *had* she been doing? Escaping the hoopla of her life?

He should have let her explain. She still deserved that, and so did he, but getting hold of a princess wasn't easy.

In fact, it was downright impossible.

He called her family compound and got the runaround. Same thing from all the businesses connected to her name. No luck with the Web sites.

If she'd had a regular address, he'd have flown there in a heartbeat, but he didn't even know where she lived.

So he called Melissa. A lot.

In the third week, Stacy got on the phone and said, "Okay, Seany, what's up?"

"Can't a guy just call his niece?"

"You really miss her?"

She sounded so surprised, he laughed. "Yeah, I really miss her. Actually, I was thinking I could come get her tomorrow and take her out for pizza."

"She's available." Stacy went quiet for a moment. "Is there something else you want to tell me? Something you want to talk about?"

"Like?"

"Like this sudden need to have people around you."

"I always like having you around."

"This is me, Sean. You love us, I know you do, but I also know you value your alone time. So what's changed?"

Sean looked out his kitchen window to the pool. He thought of Carly sitting on the edge, watching him swim.

It had all started there.

Actually, it had started the moment he'd opened his front door to her, when she'd answered his ad.

His ad.

That was it! Another ad. "Stacy, I've got to go."

"But—"

"Bye."

"Sean O'Mara, don't you dare hang up! I want to know details. I want to know—"

Gently he replaced the receiver. He'd make it up to her. Later.

Desperate times called for desperate measures. Putting another want ad in his local paper was a long shot, but she'd seen it the first time, so she had to at least view various papers from around the world, right?

God, he hoped so. He drafted a new ad. And then, to be sure, he placed it in every single major newspaper in the free world.

14

AFTER A VERY LONG WEEK, Princess Carlyne—and she was finally getting used to hearing people call her that again—slipped out of her clothes and into the bathtub, grateful for some time to herself.

She took great pride in her charity benefits, of which there'd been four this week, but they weren't enough for her. France was no longer enough for her, and neither was Spain.

Truth was, she didn't have to attend each and every one of these events personally. With a computer and a phone, she could be stationed anywhere.

Even Santa Barbara, California.

Assuming, of course, she had a reason to be there. Which she didn't.

That left a little dilemma. A little dilemma that would be getting bigger and bigger, because the stick had turned blue. In all four kits she tried.

Pregnant.

Equal parts joy and terror washed through her, and she leaned back in the tub, letting the bubbles and hot water relax her. As if that were possible.

Whether Sean wanted to talk to her or not, she had to tell him.

Determined to keep relaxed, she reached for the stack of newspapers she'd left on a stool next to the tub.

The *Washington Post* didn't intrigue her. Nor did the *Los Angeles Times*. She tossed away the *New York Times*, as well, and even knowing it would kill her, she reached for the much smaller Santa Barbara paper.

The memory of Sean's nanny ad made her mouth curve and her throat burn, but as was her habit, she skimmed the columns anyway...and abruptly sat up in shock.

Her gasp echoed against the tile and bounced back to her. She jerked the paper closer and read again.

"Wanted—What I was stupid enough to let go. A warm, funny, loving, intelligent, gorgeous caretaker for my heart and soul. Come back, Carly. Please come back."

Her heart had stopped, just stopped. Now it started again with a rapid beat. Her stomach sizzled with nerves.

Or maybe that was morning sickness.

He wanted her back?

And what would he say when he learned it was no longer just her, that she was carrying a baby? *Their* baby.

SEAN STOOD by the pool. His stress level dictated a swim, but lately doing laps had lost its appeal.

Inside, his doorbell rang, and he sighed. He had no idea if it was the courier bringing him a crucial set of plans or the pizza he'd ordered, but the swim would have to wait.

Flipping through his wallet, he opened the door, distracted by the fact that he had far less cash than he thought, which meant Melissa had picked him nearly clean last night before he'd caught her playing with his wallet.

He shuddered to think of her in another few years even as he smiled fondly at her audacity. Watch out, world.

"Sean."

At the unbearably familiar, soft, feminine voice, Sean looked up, sure he'd been hearing things, because no way could Carly be standing there delivering his pizza.

No pizza, but she *was* most definitely standing there, with her sleek blond hair and gorgeous green eyes. She wore hardly any makeup, revealing her elegant, beautiful features and her clothes fit her willowy curves.

For a ridiculous moment he stared at her, certain he'd conjured her up.

She stared back.

Then normal daytime sounds broke the silence. A car revving. A bird in a tree.

Mrs. Trykowski humming from the other side of the fence, probably at this very moment climbing a tree to spy on them.

"Hi," Carly finally whispered.

"Hi," he whispered back, his voice rough with the knot of emotion stuck in his windpipe.

"You're...not wearing much."

He looked at himself and realized he stood there in only his swimming trunks.

Her eyes ran over him hungrily, like a caress, and he felt his body tighten. He was afraid to hope, was his first thought, and his second was, would she care if he just grabbed her and hauled her close?

It wasn't easy to reconcile this worldly woman, the one he'd seen on television and in the papers, with the more whimsical, earthy woman he'd lived with for weeks.

"I'm very glad to see you," he said in the understatement of the year.

She stood very, very still. "Are you sure, Sean? Because the last time I saw you, we—"

"*Very* sure." Did he invite her in, he wondered, or just ravish her on the spot, Mrs. Trykowski be damned?

Carlyne took the matter entirely out of his hands by losing all the color in her face. Weaving slightly, she reached for the doorway.

Sean tried to grab her, but she shook him off. "I'm okay."

No, she wasn't. No one that white could be okay. "What's the matter?" Urgency roughened his voice, but she didn't answer. "Carly?"

When her eyes rolled back in her head, he grabbed her.

"Don't," she murmured as he scooped her up. "I can walk." But her head lolled against his chest.

"Shh." He couldn't talk and carry her—he felt absurdly weak with worry. She'd lost weight, and right now her skin was nearly transparent.

What was wrong?

Kicking the front door shut, he stood there, reluctant to let go of her now that he finally had her in his arms.

"I'm fine," she insisted.

"Yeah. So fine, you're blacking out."

"Honest, I can walk—"

Ignoring her, he settled her on the couch.

"You're white as a ghost, Carly," he said as lightly as he could with his heart in his throat. "You look awful."

"Thanks." She closed her eyes.

"What's the matter?" He sank to his knees on the floor and put a hand on her hip. "Are you sick?"

Turning away, she curled into a little ball. Her hair fell away from her neck, making her look all the more miserable and vulnerable. "I'm just not feeling well."

"The flu?" he demanded.

"Feels like it," she muttered, and when he slid his hand up her body to feel her forehead, which was not warm, but terribly clammy, she lifted her own to cover his. "I'm sorry," she whispered, eyes still closed. "I want to talk, we *need* to talk, but…"

Her voice trailed off, and unable to help himself, he stroked his hand down her slim spine. "It's okay."

"It was a long trip, and I couldn't sleep. I'm so sorry," she whispered again, so softly he had to lean forward to hear her. "I'm so sorry about not telling you the truth, Sean.

Please forgive me. I never meant to hurt you, I just needed to escape and—"

"Shh." His throat was tight because, dammit, *he* should be the one apologizing. When she let out a little shiver, he ran for a blanket.

"Talk to me," she said softly when he covered her. "Tell me...stuff." She slurred her words, as if she was so tired she couldn't talk.

"Carly, you're scaring me. I'm going to call a doctor."

Eyes still closed, she grabbed his wrist. "No, it was a long trip, that's all. A couple of connections got canceled. I just...need to rest a moment."

He stared at her very, *very* pale face, a face he would recognize anywhere, and wondered for the thousandth time how he could have missed it. "It's okay, it can all wait."

"Talk to me," she murmured again. "Please?"

Talk to her. The chance he'd wanted. But where to start?

From the beginning.

"Well, you know about my desperate nanny ad," he said, relieved to see a ghost of a smile touch her lips, though she was careful not to move an inch otherwise.

Sinking to the floor at her side, he stroked

her hair from her face. "At first, I didn't know what to expect. I just wanted someone to take Melissa off my hands."

She made a noise that perfectly conveyed sympathy—for Melissa.

"I know," he said shaking his head at himself. "I was a terrible uncle. All that mattered was being able to work. But work was my life, Carly, it was all that I had, all that ever mattered."

"It's okay," she whispered. "I know."

"No, it's not okay. I let you and Melissa think you weren't as important as my work. My family...they were all workaholics, you see, and that's what I learned. Work, work, work. That only success matters. But they were wrong, Carly. Very wrong."

She was so still, and again he slid his hand down her body, the warm curves so familiar he ached. She stirred slightly, arching into his hand, wordlessly telling him how much she liked his touch.

"Melissa didn't care about my work," he said quietly. "She just wanted me. *Me*," he said, marveling, shaking his head with wonder. "And then you came into our lives like a whirlwind...." He stared at his hand on her narrow waist. "I took one look at you,

Carly, and knew. I knew what you would mean to me, and it scared me to death."

She remained perfectly still, eyes closed.

"*Everything* about you scared me to death," he admitted softly. "That's why I didn't let you explain, because if I did, I'd have to understand, and if I understood that, I'd have to go the rest of the way and admit the truth." He held his breath, waiting for a sign that this was something she'd wanted to hear.

But she didn't move.

"I fell in love with you, Carly."

She was utterly, completely still, and so was his heart.

"It's not some line," he said quickly. "Believe me, I've never felt like this before."

Still nothing.

And he was dying. "Carly? Are you still upset? I want to hear what you have to say, but I want you to know it doesn't matter, none of it. I'll feel this way about you for the rest of my life, no matter what."

Not even a tremor.

Surging to his knees, he bent over her, needing a response, even if it was for her to laugh in his face. He got a response all right—a soft snuffle. A snore.

She'd fallen fast and deep asleep.

15

ASLEEP! Sitting on his heels, Sean had to let out a choked laugh. He'd just poured his heart out for the first time ever, telling a woman his true feelings, and she'd slept through the entire thing.

Definitely tough on the ego.

Carly was on her side, facing away from him, but he couldn't miss how exhausted she was. It showed in every line of the body he'd missed so much.

She wasn't well, and no matter what she said, it worried him. There were shadows under her eyes, marring her pale skin. One of her hands was tucked beneath her cheek. The other covered her belly in a protective gesture that told him she must have a stomachache. Probably the flu, the poor baby. Her breathing came deep and slow, her mouth in a stressed frown that tore at him.

He was dying to know what had brought her back. Had she missed him? Was it possible? Or had his ad brought her here? But everything would have to wait.

"It's okay," he whispered, leaning close to softly kiss her temple. "Sleep. Get better. Everything else can wait."

At that, she let out a shuddering sigh, and her entire body relaxed. Then her hand, the one clutched to her belly, unfisted as she fell into deeper sleep. And out of her fingers fell a folded piece of paper.

He unfolded the torn, dog-eared piece of newsprint, and his heart caught yet again.

It was his ad.

CARLY AWOKE SLOWLY, purposely lying completely still, having gotten used to her world spinning out of control for those first few shaky moments of awareness.

Then she remembered. She wasn't at home in her own bed, where she could reach for crackers and feel the overwhelming loneliness that life had brought in the past few weeks.

She remembered the ad, remembered grabbing nothing more than her purse and racing for the airport. She remembered calling Francesca from her cell phone with a brief explanation and being cheerfully told to "go for it".

She remembered having to make several connections, fearing she'd never make it. It had been a nightmare. She hadn't been able to eat properly, and all the stress had sapped her strength.

By the time she'd shown up on Sean's doorstep, she'd been only a moment away from passing out, and humiliating as it had been, she'd never been happier to see anyone in her entire life.

Then she'd fallen asleep on him.

She'd been all set to woo Sean, to do whatever it took to make him happy about the baby, and what had she done?

Passed out cold.

She groaned, and a firm, warm hand slid over her cheek. "Ah, she lives," his deep voice was very close.

She could hear relief, anxiety and something more, so she opened her eyes to be sure, and yes, he was smiling at her, but she didn't know if it was because she was there, or if he was just happy she hadn't thrown up on him.

Then she realized she was in his spare bedroom, and the wee light coming through the windows looked suspiciously like early morning light. Had she—

"Yep. Slept all night," he told her. "Just like a baby."

Her gaze jerked to his. *Did he know?*

"I made you some tea because I didn't know if you'd want to eat. The flu, I'd guess?"

She could eat a horse, she was so ravenous. And if she didn't eat soon, she'd turn green again, and maybe throw up on him, after all.

"Have you been sick long?"

"No," she said, her voice husky from the first good night's sleep she'd had since she left California.

He hadn't taken her to *his* bedroom last night, she noticed, which made her wonder if she'd somehow missed the meaning of his ad.

How to tell him? Where to start? The love part, she decided, she'd start with the love part. Holding her breath, she stared at him, hoping she wouldn't ruin everything by blurting it out, that he wouldn't feel trapped. "Sean..."

"Carly." A teasing light came into his eyes. "We remember each others' names. That's nice."

When she didn't return the smile, his

faded. "I'm sorry. I make stupid jokes when I'm nervous."

She gaped at him. "Why are *you* nervous?"

"I'm thinking that any second here you're going to tell me you've got to go."

It was the opening she needed, and she fumbled for the newspaper clipping she'd been holding, but it wasn't in her hands or by her bed.

"Is this what you're looking for?" He held out the tattered ad.

She took it, though she had the words memorized. "You asked me to come back," she whispered, clutching it to her chest.

"Yes."

"To be the caretaker of your heart and soul."

"Yes."

"Oh, Sean. I can't keep this in anymore." She spoke at the speed of light before she could lose her nerve. "I was dying for you. I know you never wanted another commitment, but I've never been as happy as I was taking care of Melissa and being with you. I don't want to scare you off, or ruin anything, and I don't know why you wrote that ad, but the truth is—" She drew in a long, hard breath. "I love you." The air whooshed out of her, and though it was hard to talk without breathing, she couldn't draw another breath. "I love you more than I've ever loved anyone."

He reached out and cupped her face. "Oh, Carly."

She closed her eyes. "I'm sorry, I couldn't keep it in any longer, even if you don't feel the same way. And that's not all, Sean, I've—"

"I love you, too," he said, eyes shining. "I told you so last night, sweetheart. If you hadn't fallen asleep on me, you would have heard it yourself."

Her heart surged painfully against the walls of her chest. For a second she was afraid she'd heard him wrong, but his smile was different, special, and those eyes of his were wet. "You love me," she whispered, touching his face.

"Yes, with all my heart and soul. I've been trying to reach you. You're harder to get ahold of than the President."

"Is...is that why you placed the ad?"

He stretched out beside her, pulled her close. "Pretty desperate, huh?"

"I loved it." She had to laugh. "I can't believe it. The most wonderful man in the world tells me he loves me, and I sleep through it." She pulled back. "There's a reason I was so sleepy, Sean."

"You've been sick."

"No. Well, yes, but it's not what you think."

He sobered quickly, and if she thought his eyes brilliant before, it was nothing to what happened now. "What's wrong?"

"Sean, I want to live with you."

"Yes. God, yes."

Her breath caught at the vehemence in his voice. "Here, in Santa Barbara."

"I want to marry you, Carly. I don't care where. I just want to be with you. Now tell me what's wrong."

"I miss Melissa," she blurted. "She should be here."

"We'll call her. And someday we'll have our own family. Now tell me what's the matter."

She covered her mouth as a laugh escaped, then swiped at her sudden tears.

"Carly, you're terrifying me." With a gentleness that only caused more tears, he slid his thumb over her cheek, catching a teardrop. "Please, tell me."

"Well...about that someday child thing." She meant to laugh but cried instead. "It's not so far down the road."

His hand went still on her face. "You mean…"

"Yes." Taking his other hand, she placed it on her belly. "We can have it all right now," she whispered, her voice cracking at the look of utter love and heat and fascination in his gaze. "Heart and soul."

"Heart and soul," he repeated, kissing her hard. "Heart and soul."

Silhouette Books invites you to cherish
a captivating keepsake collection by

DIANA PALMER

They're rugged and lean…and the best-looking, sweetest-talking men in the Lone Star State! CALHOUN, JUSTIN and TYLER—the three mesmerizing cowboys who started the legend. Now they're back by popular demand in one classic volume—ready to lasso your heart!

You won't want to miss this treasured collection from international bestselling author Diana Palmer!

LONG, TALL Texans

CALHOUN, JUSTIN & TYLER
(On sale March 2002)

Available at your favorite retail outlet.

Silhouette®
Where love comes alive™